HER REBEL COWBOY

STEPHANIE ROWE

HER REBEL COWBOY

Copyright © 2017 by Stephanie Rowe

ISBN-10: 1-940968-51-8
ISBN-13: 978-1-940968-51-3

For further information, please contact:
Stephanie@stephanierowe.com

Dedication

To Guinevere Jones. Without you, this book never would have been written, and you know it! I love you, babe!

Acknowledgements

Special thanks to my core team of amazing people, without whom I would never have been able to create this book. Each of you is so important, and your contribution was exactly what I needed. I'm so grateful to all of you! Your emails of support, or yelling at me because I hadn't sent you more of the book yet, or just your advice on covers, back cover copy and all things needed to whip this book into shape—every last one of them made a difference to me. I appreciate each one of you so much! I want to give a huge shout out to all my beta readers, whose eagle eyes and late night reading helped whip this book into shape. You guys are the BEST! Special thanks to the Rockstars. There are so many to thank by name, more than I could count, but here are those who I want to called out specially for all they did to help this book come to life: Malinda Davis Diehl, Leslie Barnes, Kayla Bartley, Alencia Bates Salters, Alyssa Bird, Donna Bossert, Jean Bowden, Shell Bryce, Kelley Daley Curry, Ashley Cuesta, Denise Fluhr, Valerie Glass, Heidi Hoffman, Jeanne Stone, Dottie Jones, Janet Juengling-Snell, Deb Julienne, Bridget Koan, Felicia Low, Helen Loyal, Phyllis Marshall, Suzanne Mayer, Jodi Moore, Ashlee Murphy, Elizabeth Neal, Judi Pflughoeft, Carol Pretorius, Kasey Richardson, Caryn Santee, Amber Ellison Shriver, Summer Steelman, Regina Thomas, and Linda Watson. Special thanks to my family, who I love with every fiber of my heart and soul. And to AER, who is my world. Love you so much, baby girl! And to my beloved Joe, who shows me daily what romance is really about.

Chapter 1

A T ANY MOMENT, Wyatt Parker was going to find out what happened three hours ago. He wasn't going to lie. He was scared shitless to get that call—

The bull he was riding jumped to the left, jerking Wyatt off balance. He lost his grip and was ripped over the bull's right shoulder. Swearing, he ducked his head a split second before he hit the ground, face planting into the dirt.

The shock of the crash on his not-quite-healed body kept him motionless for a moment while he waited for the impact to stop reverberating through him. As he lay there, spitting dirt, he realized that he'd missed even the taste of dirt during his two-month suspension.

After endlessly waking up in the middle of the night, sweating his ass off from another nightmare that he was never going to get on another bull again...he was suddenly days away from competition again...or from being banned for life, like his old man.

Banned for life. The words made an icy chill grip his spine. *Banned for life* from the only thing that made his heart beat. Sweat broke out on his brow, but it wasn't from the pain of his crash. It was from the raw terror of having bull riding taken away from him.

He wasn't a praying man, but hell, he'd even thrown up a couple requests to that big, blue western Oregon sky to make sure he covered all his bases. The World Rodeo Championships rules committee was reviewing his appeal today. He knew he was innocent, but he also knew that didn't always matter. According to what he'd heard, the decision had been scheduled to come down three hours ago. His fate was already sealed. All that was left was for someone to tell him what had happened.

Unless the majority of that committee believed his innocence, everything that mattered to him was going to be stripped away from him because of one eight-second ride two months ago.

Eight damn seconds.

"Get up, Wyatt! Hell, man, get up!"

Awareness came roaring back to him, and Wyatt vaulted to his feet just as the bull who'd dumped him lowered his head to impale him. Wyatt lunged to the right, and the horn clipped his right hip, knocking him off his feet. The bull's feet pounded down next to his head, and Wyatt rolled to the side as hooves thudded past him. He scrambled up and sprinted for the fence, hauling himself over the rails as the bull thundered by.

Grinning, Wyatt leaned on the rails, sweat beading down his brow. "Hell, I missed this."

"You're not ready." Brody Hart, who'd been his friend since they were kids, slammed the gate behind the bull, glaring at Wyatt as if it was his damn fault that the bull had almost crushed him. Which it was. He'd had no business taking his time getting up, and they both knew it.

Brody didn't ride the bulls, claiming that bull riding was for assholes who wanted fame, money, and chicks. He stuck with the horses, and the proof of his success was the expansive neighboring ranch he owned with his seven brothers and two sisters, none of whom were related by blood or even paperwork, but were the most loyal family he'd ever known in his life.

Wyatt had always thought he'd had a messed-up childhood...until he'd met Brody and the rest of the Harts, when they were all teenagers. Back then, the Hart clan had been nothing more than a desperate, scared bunch of runaways living under a bridge in downtown Portland, Oregon, hiding from authorities who wanted to drag them back into the assorted hells that they'd escaped from. The group of runaways had taken the same last name in an attempt to make it more difficult for anyone to pry them apart. They'd trusted no one but themselves...and Wyatt, eventually. Wyatt wasn't a Hart, but the time he'd spent living under that bridge with them, fighting for food and survival, had created a bond that would last forever.

And now Brody was giving him that same look he'd given Wyatt the day he'd said he wanted to ride bulls in the first place, the look that said he was such a stupid ass that it wasn't even worth talking to him.

Man, he loved Brody.

Wyatt grinned. "Shut the hell up, bro." Shaking out the aches from hitting the dirt, Wyatt straightened up, and finished climbing the rails. "I'm fine."

"That bull has been retired for three years," Brody said, watching him through narrowed eyes. "Even I could ride that senior citizen with no hands and blindfolded, but he dumped you on your ass. How's that fine, exactly? Because I'm a little unclear on that logic."

"Just lost my grip on the rope." Wyatt pulled off his helmet. "You know I step up in competition. I'm just feeling my seat."

Brody stared at him. "You were paralyzed less than two months ago. There's no way you should be on a bull already."

Wyatt tensed. "I was paralyzed for only a few hours. I'm fine."

"Bullshit. You don't have your rhythm. I can tell your neck still hurts, and you can't breathe half the time from those damn broken ribs that aren't completely healed. And how's that head? Bet you're seeing stars after that hit you just took."

"My head's fine." Yeah, he'd gotten a slight concussion during his last ride a couple months ago, but it wasn't enough to stop him. He would have been back on the circuit the next weekend if he hadn't been suspended. *Suspended.* Damn.

Brody narrowed his eyes, seeing more than Wyatt was telling him, as he always did. Growing up on the streets, you either got fucked over, or you learned to be the smartest, most observant badass that ever lived. Brody was the latter, and although it had protected the others that had come to him for aid, it was also annoying as hell at times.

"You're riding like shit." Brody clearly decided stating the blatantly obvious was worth his time. It wasn't. "If it's not your head, what's going on?"

"Just rusty." Wyatt had started riding a couple days ago when he'd gotten the news that his appeal was going to be heard this week, determined to be ready if he were reinstated. He'd been pumped to get back on, but it had been ugly. He wasn't going to admit it, but Brody was right. He had no feel for the bull at all. It was like he was no longer connected to the animals that had been a part of his life since he was a teenager. He couldn't figure out what he was doing wrong, and he was running out of time to get his shit together. Three days, to be exact...assuming the committee ruled in his favor.

Which they had to. He was innocent, and they'd see it.

Except he knew damn well that they might not. Innocent people didn't always get cleared, especially when they were the son of the most notorious bull rider who had ever tarnished the sport.

Brody studied him intensely. "The docs say you could die if you get hit like that again."

Yeah, he knew that, and it didn't matter. "Every bull rider could die any time they go out there. It's better to die doing what you love, than spend a life hiding in a cave."

Brody whistled softly. "Hang it up, man. You've had the career. It's not worth it."

Shit. It was so much more complicated than that. "Yeah? You think I should retire? And then what? What the hell else would I do if I walked away?"

"Take Bunny up on her offer to buy this ranch. Turn it into what it's supposed to be." Brody grinned. "Ranch life is good, bro. You'd like it. This place has potential, and if her nephew buys the place, he's going to turn it into some glitzy resort for Hollywood celebs who want to get away from LA. All this will be lost."

Wyatt instinctively glanced at the white ranch house at the top of the hill, the one owned by Bunny Hickerson. He'd known Bunny almost his entire life, and he lived in her bunk house in exchange for running the place since her husband had died a few years back. She was the one who'd given him the chance that had gotten him off the streets, and he'd taken care of her ever since.

But things were changing. Now that her husband was

gone, Bunny was ready to retire to Cape Cod, a place she'd always loved. She was putting Sleeping Bull Ranch on the market at the end of the month...which both pissed him off and relieved him.

Once she sold the ranch, Wyatt would no longer be tethered to it. He'd be free to go wherever he wanted and ride bulls until it killed him...which was good. But at the same time, the Hickerson ranch called to him. It felt like the home he'd never had. Shuffled around from relative to relative while his dad was on the WRC tour or in jail, Wyatt had never lived more than a few months in one place as a kid, except the year he'd spent with the Harts. Bunny's place was the first place he'd lived for any length of time, and it had been his anchor ever since.

He liked coming back here after a competition. He liked making sure things ran smoothly. He took pride in the bulls they bred, in seeing Hickerson bulls on the circuit and knowing he had a hand in it. Yeah, it was a small operation, but the baseline was solid. But to own it? To get up in the same place, from the same bed, every damn day for the rest of his life? To be *responsible* for the ranch? No chance. He knew it wasn't his thing. Never would be. He simply wasn't cut out for it. "I don't want it."

Brody sighed. "You want Nathan to get it? Turn it into a resort?"

Wyatt grimaced at the mention of Bunny's relentless nephew. "She won't sell it to him."

"He'll find a way to get it, if for no other reason than to make sure you don't get it. He hates that you're the one she likes."

Wyatt shrugged. "I'm not going to buy the ranch just to block him. Bunny will handle him. She's smart. I'm going back on the tour."

Brody shook his head. "Don't be an ass. Take a lesson

from your dad and know when to stop."

Wyatt tensed at Brody's comment, at the reminder of the legacy that haunted him, the one he'd been trying to outrun for twenty years. The one that had come back to bite him in the ass two months ago. His dad, who had cheated, refused to accept his lifetime ban, and then drank himself to death in misery. "Screw that. No way. I'm getting back on the tour."

He couldn't walk away now. He'd fought against his dad's reputation his whole life, and he'd nearly gotten people to forget about it...until two months ago. His bull in the finals had been an absolute beast, giving Wyatt the highest score in history, and a wreck that had nearly broken his body for good. That ride had made him a legend...until it had been discovered that his bull had been drugged into a rage that had resulted in that high score.

The blame had instantly landed on Wyatt's shoulders, as a cheat, just like his old man, and the suspension had come down the next day, while he'd been lying in the hospital.

And now, he needed to prove that he wasn't a cheater, and the only way to do that was to win clean. "I'm going back on the tour, Brody. Drop it. Let's bring another bull in." He swung his leg over the fence and dropped down to the parched earth that was so starved for rain. He glanced at the dark clouds rolling in the distance, calculating how much time they had before the bad weather took over. "I want to get a couple more rides in before the storm hits."

"No."

Wyatt glanced at his friend as he reached the gate. "No, what?"

"No." Brody walked over. "No, I'm not going to help you ride. I've been your friend for too long, Wyatt. I've been watching you ride for two days now, and you're out of sync. You're still hurting from your crash, and your game is off. You don't have it right, and you're gonna get hurt. Bad hurt. Just to prove to a bunch of assholes that you're not a cheat? Well, screw them. It's not worth your life. I can't stop you from riding, but I'll be damned if I'll help you write your own death ticket." He looked at Wyatt. "Brothers tell each other when they're being stupid, so I'm telling you now. You're being stupid."

Wyatt's chest tightened at the brother reference, as it always did. He wasn't a Hart, but he loved that clan as his own family. But that didn't mean they didn't piss him off sometimes. "Brody, I can't practice without you–"

"I know. That's why I'm not helping. See ya, bro." Brody turned to walk toward his truck, then paused, looking toward the left, toward the ranch house.

At the same moment, Wyatt heard the crunch of boots, and he glanced in the same direction Brody was looking. A tall, lean cowboy in a black cowboy hat and jeans was striding down toward the ring from the main house. He recognized him immediately as Jesse Knight, one of the Knight brothers. Jesse's grandfather had founded the World Rodeo Championships circuit, and he and a couple of his brothers owned a detective agency that often assisted the circuit.

Wyatt tensed at the sight of Jesse approaching. Why was he there? Was this about his suspension? There was only one reason he could think of for one of the Knight brothers to be coming here, and that was if there was something out of the ordinary with the ruling on his suspension.

Shit. Wyatt had been so certain he'd be cleared. The presence of Jesse Knight meant he was wrong.

Dead wrong.

And he was about to find out why.

Chapter 2

S WEARING, WYATT HEADED toward the fence, meeting Jesse as he walked up. "Jesse."

"Wyatt." The two men shook hands.

Wyatt stepped back restlessly, not in the mood for meaningless platitudes. "What's up?" He didn't bother with preambles. Only one thing mattered, and that was getting back in the ring. "You're here about the suspension? My appeal didn't go through?"

Jesse tipped his hat back. "Someone juiced that bull you rode."

Wyatt nodded. "I know. It wasn't me." He was aware of Brody walking up to stand beside him, covering his back. Always loyal, even when he was irritated with him. Wyatt fucking loved the Harts. They'd taught him about loyalty when he hadn't even had the first clue what it meant. He'd go through hell and back for every single one of them.

Jesse studied him. "The chemical in the bull's system

wasn't designed to give you a ride tough enough to give you a high score. It was meant to get you killed."

Wyatt blinked, startled by the announcement. "What? Kill me? What are you talking about?"

"My brother's a vet. He researched the drug. The only possible use of that drug in the quantities found in that bull's body was to make it uncontrollable, and insanely aggressive. To make its mind snap. It wasn't a fluke he went after you when you were down. If it hadn't been for the clowns, you'd be dead." Jesse cocked an eyebrow. "We also found someone had doctored the coffee of both the clowns working your ride. Neither of them had had time to drink it, but if they had, they both would have been half-asleep and too slow to help you when the bull went after you. It was a setup, Wyatt. An assassination."

Sudden tension gripped Wyatt's shoulders. He could tell from Jesse's face that he was dead serious. "What the hell?"

Beside him, Brody shifted, and Wyatt could feel the tension rolling off him. "Someone tried to murder Wyatt? You think Wyatt was the specific target, or did he just happen to be in the wrong place?"

Jesse glanced at him, his face solemn. "The bull was drugged *after* Wyatt was announced as his rider. Wyatt was the target."

Shit. "That makes no sense. Who the hell would want to kill me?" And why? But even as he asked, a name popped into his head. He swore. Shit. No. It was impossible.

He glanced at Brody, who looked as stunned as Wyatt felt. *Murder?* What the hell?

Jesse shrugged. "I don't know who did it, but that's why I'm here. You got any ideas?"

"No–"

"Yes, you do." Brody interrupted. "You're thinking

the same thing I'm thinking."

"Who?" Jesse asked.

Wyatt looked at Brody. "She would never try to kill me–"

"Who?" Jesse repeated the question.

Wyatt looked at Brody for a long moment, then Brody turned to Jesse. "Octavia Kincaid. Wyatt's former fiancée."

A hard, cold sensation settled in Wyatt's gut, that same coldness that had gripped him since the day he'd learned of her betrayal a year ago. He couldn't even hear her name without all the feelings of that moment crashing down upon him.

Jesse raised his brows. "I thought it was an amicable breakup."

"No way," Brody muttered. "She–"

"Enough." Wyatt cut off his friend. There was no way he was going there. She wasn't worth it. Instead, he focused on what mattered to him. "What about the suspension? It's cleared, then?"

Brody swore. "Hell, Wyatt. Let go of the riding. That doesn't matter right now."

"It matters." Wyatt kept his gaze on Jesse. "Well?"

Jesse nodded. "Yeah, you're clear."

"Hell." Relief rushed over Wyatt, so intense that he had to clench his fist. His name was *cleared*. "So, I can ride this weekend?"

Brody swore again. "You're not ready."

Jesse was shaking his head. "Someone tried to kill you. If you go back out there now, before we figure it out, they could get it right this time. Stay low. Keep recovering. Give me a few days to figure it out. I'll need more information on the situation with Octavia, and any other names." He assessed Wyatt carefully. "And how in the hell did you get medical clearance to ride, anyway? I saw that crash. You should be sidelined."

"I'm fine." Had Octavia really tried to kill him? That made no sense. "I don't think Octavia would try to kill me, but I don't know of anyone else. I have no clue." And he didn't. He couldn't even wrap his mind around the fact that someone had tried to kill him. "If it was Octavia, she didn't try to kill me. Jeopardize my ride? Yeah, sure. I could buy that, and there are a few other names I could list." He dropped a few names of competitors who hadn't liked Wyatt's fast rise to the top. "But try murder? No way. No one." But even as he said it, he flashed back to that night a year ago, when the woman he'd trusted, who he'd thought he'd loved, had ripped apart everything that had mattered to him, everything that he'd built up. Octavia had taught him never to trust a woman again, and it was a lesson he was never going to forget.

Jesse met his gaze. "Someone tried to murder you, Wyatt. Accept it, and stay off the bulls this weekend, until I figure it out."

"Stay off the bulls?" Wyatt glanced back over his shoulder at the ring. At the dirt. He was supposed to walk away because some piece of shit tried to take him down? No. Never. He turned back "No chance. I need to ride." He saw the resistance on the faces of both men, but it didn't matter. He had to ride. He knew he had no choice. For reasons that no one but him would ever understand.

Some choices weren't really choices. Some choices were simply fate, burned into a man's bones, a destiny from which there was no deviation, no reprieve, and no salvation.

He was going to ride this weekend. If he died, well, he died. He accepted that possibility. Death had never scared him. It was failing to claim the life he was meant to live that haunted him.

Chapter 3

NOELLE WILDER GRIMACED when she saw her best friend reach for the handle of her fridge. "I haven't been grocery shopping for a while," she warned, trying to preempt the lecture that would be coming as soon as Kate saw the contents.

"Holy crap, girl." Kate Jackson stared into the fridge, her upper lip curling in horror. "Expired eggs, curdled milk, and a plastic container full of something so old I can't even tell what it once was? That's it? That's all you have in here? How do you survive on that? And more importantly, how on earth is that going to inspire a culinary mystery worthy of the hundred thousand copies your last one sold?"

"As soon as the chocolate starts to melt on the stove, the scent will inspire me." Ignoring her throbbing headache, Noelle stared at the computer screen, willing her brain to start working again, for those long-absent ideas to begin to flow.

"No, it won't." Kate slammed the fridge shut. "Face it, girlfriend. Chocolate can't help you this time."

"Of course it can. Chocolate can salvage anything– Hey!" Kate snatched the computer from her lap.

Noelle sighed and glared at her friend. "Really, Kate? How's that helpful?"

"Because staring at blinking cursors on a blank screen for hours on end has been documented to rot the brain cells, and you need all the ones you can still salvage." Kate set the computer on the kitchen counter. "Face it, Noelle. You've even killed chocolate."

Noelle raised her eyebrows. "No one can kill chocolate." Although, if she was honest with herself, she had to acknowledge the truth that if anyone could kill chocolate, she had a feeling that it might be her.

"No?" Kate leaned forward. "Then tell me, what's the first thing that comes to your mind when I mention a very sharp dagger hidden in a molten chocolate lava cake?"

The image of her bed and her favorite fuzzy blanket popped into her head...and that was just not a good thing for a culinary mystery writer. "Oh, God. I didn't see any blood," she said, staring at Kate in horror. "No dead bodies. It makes me want to crawl into my bed and take a nap instead of dealing with it."

Kate sighed and sat down next to her. "You didn't have any visions of what kind of deranged villain would put a dagger in a dessert?"

Noelle groaned. "No. My brain feels like it ran into hiding when I tried to picture the dagger." She closed her eyes and let her head drop back against the couch, suddenly feeling too tired to cope. "That's it then, isn't it? That's what you've been trying to tell me. I can't do this anymore."

"That's exactly what I've been trying to tell you,"

Kate said gently. "You're dying inside Noelle. Can't you feel it?"

Weariness seemed to strip Noelle of the last vestiges of her enthusiasm, but she opened her eyes and made herself sit straighter. "Don't say that. You don't know what it's like to die. The fact I'm tired isn't the same thing at all–"

"Don't start that with me," Kate snapped. "I know that you spent years trying to keep David from dying. I know you lived that, and I know how much it sucked to spend the first three years of your marriage watching your husband die. I get that. I was here, remember? However, I'm not talking about a physical death, and you know it. I'm talking about your soul, your heart, your spirit."

Noelle bit her lip at the sudden burn of tears in her eyes. "I'm okay," she said stubbornly. "I really am–"

"Sweetie, you've spent the year since David's death trying to keep his dream alive, and it's killing you. Just because he died doesn't mean you have to, as well."

Noelle lifted her chin. "I made him a promise to help his brother and keep his restaurant going. I mean, our restaurant. We opened it together, and it was his dream, I mean, our dream. Don't you remember that? Or did you forget that part?"

"Oh, I remember when you guys decided to open it. I remember when you guys fell in love over the stove. But I also remember when you used to lose yourself in your stories and write until your face glowed with joy, while he pulled most of the weight in the kitchen. I don't see any joy anymore. When was the last time you felt joy?"

"I–" Noelle's voice faded as she tried to remember. She couldn't even remember what joy felt like. All she could feel, all she'd felt for ages, was a tightness in her chest, and a numbness that made every moment and every day the same, day after day after day. No joy. No pain.

Just an empty numbness propelled by obligation.

Kate sighed. "Sweetie, David loved the restaurant, but he loved you more. The last thing he would've wanted was for you to live like this, so broken and empty. That restaurant was *his* dream. You did it because you loved him, but when he was alive, you were able to spend a lot of time writing. Now you're there all the time, fighting for a dream that isn't yours. You can't keep doing both."

"Of course I can." Noelle shoved herself to her feet and padded across her bare wood floor to the stove, where the chocolate was beginning to melt perfectly.

"Can you?" Kate didn't bother to keep the skepticism out of her voice. "This book you're working on was due how long ago? How many extensions have you gotten?"

Noelle grabbed a wooden spoon and began to stir the chocolate, watching the rich, creamy substance swirl in her pot. She used to love watching it swirl. Now? She felt nothing. God. When was the last time she felt anything? The day David died. She'd felt something then, but ever since? Nothing. Just endless numbness. "My editor understands."

"I'm sure she does, but she's going to stick around for only so long if you don't deliver. You're a year late on your book, Noelle. A *year*."

"I know!" Noelle set the spoon down. "I'm trying!"

"I know you are, babe, but it's not working, is it?"

Noelle leaned against the kitchen counter and looked at her friend. Suddenly, the weight of the last four years seemed to overwhelm her, and she felt exhausted. "So, maybe I shouldn't write anymore. Maybe I should just go full-time at the restaurant."

Kate's eyebrows shot up. "Really? *That's* your plan? Give up on the one thing that makes you happy, so you can work at a restaurant that's draining your energy and savings? Because that sounds like a fulfilling and brilliant way to spend the rest of your life."

Noelle gritted her teeth, her fingers digging into the counter. "What am I supposed to do? Walk away? Then what happens to Joel? He's the only family David has left, and I promised I'd make sure he was okay. If I close the restaurant, what will happen to him? We both know the only reason he's been sober the last two years is because the restaurant gives him purpose."

Kate shrugged. "So give it to him, then. He's a great chef. He'd be thrilled."

"Give it to Joel? Just walk away from it completely?" Guilt tore through her, a deep, anguished guilt because, for a split second, she'd wanted to cry with relief at the idea of doing that. But how could she? She couldn't. "He needs me to run it. He's a chef, not a business person."

"Let him hire a business manager."

"There's not enough money for that–"

"For heaven's sake, Noelle! Do you hear yourself? You're doing the job for free and putting your own money into it, just because you've convinced yourself that Joel, who's a great chef and has been sober for two years, can't manage without you. Does he really need you? Maybe he needs you to get the hell out of his life so he can stop being David's little brother and find his own strength. Did that ever occur to you?"

Noelle felt like her head was going to explode. She was suddenly too exhausted to cope. "David was the only safe space I ever had in my life, Kate. I won't betray that, or him, or his brother, regardless of the cost to me. This is what I was meant to do. It matters to me. David would've done the same for me."

Kate's face softened. "I know he would have, but would you have ever asked him to give up his dreams until he had no spirit left?"

Noelle stared at her friend. "Of course not. Never."

"So, why is it okay for you to sacrifice yourself that way?"

"I..." Noelle didn't have an answer. Suddenly, it was just too difficult to understand. "I don't know. It just is."

Kate sighed. "Okay, let me present this another way. Maybe you want to sacrifice yourself. That's your choice. But if your goal is to always have a place for Joel to work, you're going to fail there as well. The way it's going now, the restaurant will fail without your supplemental income, but if you don't write a great book soon, you won't have the money to fund it. At the very least, admit that."

Noelle tensed, her stomach clenched with sharp pains as Kate voiced the fear that haunted her day and night. "I know," she whispered. It was very possible that she was going to run out of money. She was already living on savings, and without another book in the pipeline, she was going to be in deep trouble, and then she could do nothing for Joel or David. "I can't fix that, Kate. I can't write anymore. I've tried. I really have." The admission burned as she voiced the fear that had been haunting her constantly for so long. "I can't write anymore." God. It was out there. Acknowledged. *I can't write anymore.*

Kate held up her hand. "No. You can write. It's just that your soul is withering, and you can't write without it. You have to find your muse again, and it has to be now. Or there's going to be nothing left of your soul to call upon."

"My soul?" She wanted to protest, to claim Kate was being melodramatic, but there were some times, in the middle of the night, when she couldn't sleep, that it *did* feel like her soul was withering. The aching, empty void inside her seemed to be growing deeper with every passing day, no matter how hard she tried.

"Yes. You've shut down your soul, and that's just not going to work for a woman whose career depends on baring her rawest emotions on the page. Something has to change."

"I know." Noelle couldn't deny it anymore. "You're right. But what? I don't know what to do."

"I know you don't, but lucky for you, I do." Kate smiled, but there was a fire in her eyes, a gleam of excitement that made Noelle stiffen.

She knew Kate too well not to be afraid of that gleam, and she realized suddenly that the entire conversation had been a clever, well-orchestrated manipulation to back her into the exact corner she was in. She set down the spoon and stared at her friend. "Oh, God, Kate. What have you done?"

Kate didn't even try to look innocent. "Do you know what a house swap is?"

Noelle narrowed her eyes. "You mean, when one person trades two weeks in their New York City condo with someone who has a ski chalet in Colorado? So they live in each other's houses for two weeks?"

"Exactly," Kate pulled a thick, manila envelope out of her purse and slapped it onto the counter. "Girl, you're going to cowboy country. One month on the Sleeping Bull Ranch in Eastern Oregon."

"A ranch?" For one fraction of a millisecond, an image of a sexy, seductive cowboy flashed in Noelle's mind, the same image that she'd fantasized about since she'd been sixteen years old, and read her first cowboy Harlequin romance novel on a sleepover with Kate. Excitement rushed through her, but it was chased away instantly by the reality of her situation. She shook her head. "A month? There's no way. I have to run the restaurant, and I have this deadline. And—"

"You don't have a choice. Remember that whole

'house swap' concept? Well, the owner of Sleeping Bull Ranch, Bunny Hickerson, is going to be living in your lovely Boston abode for the next month. She arrives tomorrow at noon. You don't have anywhere else to live."

Noelle's jaw dropped open. "What? You rented my apartment? Are you crazy? You don't have the right to do that—"

"Oh, but I do. Remember how you and I lived here before you got married? Well, guess who did the automatic renewal every year without bothering to update the name on it? Yes, that would be you, my absent-minded creative friend. I'm still on the lease, so yeah, I can. I did. You don't have a home for four weeks starting tomorrow at noon."

Shock numbed Noelle at Kate's announcement. She didn't know how to respond. A part of her wanted to argue and shut down the entire idea immediately. But at the same time, a deeper part of her that wanted to grab the envelope and run, away from her deadline, away from the restaurant, away from the memories that wouldn't let her go. But she didn't move. How could she take off and go to Oregon? She had obligations. Deadlines. People counting on her.

There was no way she could accept the offer, no matter how badly a part of her burned to do just that.

So, instead of grabbing it, she bit her lip and went back to stirring. "Thanks for trying, but I can't leave. The restaurant and my deadline–"

"Wrong." Kate grinned and pushed the envelope closer, sliding it across the counter toward Noelle. "You aren't accomplishing anything here, my friend, and it's not getting better. Take a few weeks off. Find your spirit. Awaken your muse, and find your own space again."

"But–"

"I'll pop in on Joel every few days just to check on

everything, so there's nothing at the restaurant for you to worry about. So, go."

Noelle stared at the envelope, sudden longing surging inside her. How amazing did it sound to get away for a month? To just walk away from all the weight that had been getting so heavy? She bit her lip, guilt rushing through her. "I can't—"

"You can." Kate leaned forward. "And you have to. You're wrecking your career, and the restaurant. You have to step back, Noelle. You have to find you again. It's time." Kate picked up the envelope and held it out. "Just take it, girl. Go find yourself again."

Longing coursed through Noelle, but she didn't move. "I can't just walk away from my life, Kate–"

"Do you want to stay here? Or do you want to get the hell out of here and breathe again?"

Noelle looked around the tiny apartment that she'd been trapped in for the last four years. Three years, taking care of David, and then this last year, fighting with the computer, trying desperately to write. Suddenly, it felt so small and oppressive, a prison crushing her. She thought of the restaurant, of walking in there night after night, knowing that it was sliding into failure, and she couldn't stop it. "Yes," she whispered, barely able to acknowledge the truth even to herself. "I can't keep living like this."

"I know, babe." Kate held out the envelope. "Take it. It's time."

Noelle stared at the envelope, then silently, her hand shaking, she held out her palm. Kate set it in her hand. The moment her fingers closed around the smooth envelope, the hugest sense of relief flooded her, and she knew it was exactly what she needed. "Thanks."

"No problem." Kate winked. "And just so you know, Bunny said the foreman on the ranch is super hot. Single, too."

Heat flooded Noelle's cheeks, and she rolled her eyes as she pressed the envelope to her chest, her heart pounding with life for the first time in so long. "Dating? No way. I've had enough of men." She pointed the envelope at her friend. "I'm going, but it's just to find my muse, not to even look at a man. The last thing I need right now is a complication."

"On the contrary, my dear," Kate said as she leaned back in the chair and beamed at her. "I think complications are exactly what you need. *Exactly* what you need."

Chapter 4

S O, YEAH, APPARENTLY there was a reason why people read novels instead of actually trying to experience the life they were reading about.

Because fantasies had no place in real life. Ever.

Especially fantasies that involved romantic, soul-enriching excursions to ranch country out west.

Noelle had been dreaming about cowboys and the Wild West since she was a kid, and not a single one of those fantasies included driving her rental car off the road and into a flooded ditch during a thunderstorm. Granted, she'd been driving slowly when she'd hit the brakes to avoid a coyote, and the slide down the embankment had been gentle and danger-free, but that didn't change the fact that her car wasn't getting back on the road by itself. And the part about not having any cell service? Yeah, that hadn't made it into even a single fantasy, and for good reason apparently.

Because it kind of sucked.

Noelle sighed, resting her wrists on the steering wheel as she watched the rain hammer onto her windshield. The din of pounding rain sounded like a herd of cattle stampeding across her metal roof, which, again, wasn't exactly how she'd envisioned her first cattle experience.

She'd been sitting in her car for two hours and six minutes, and not a single car had driven by. Not one. She was on some dirt road, not that far from her destination, and apparently, none of the other residents of Eastern Oregon had any business along this particular stretch of road.

So, yay for finding a place where she wasn't going to be harassed by having to deal with people, right? Go her.

She glanced at the dashboard on her car. Almost seven o'clock. It would be getting dark soon, and she so didn't want to spend the night here. She looked again at her directions. How much farther could the ranch be? She was almost there. She could sit there in the car until someone found her clean-picked skeleton, or she could use her body that she was lucky enough to have, and hike the rest of the distance.

The idea of hiking made energy hum through her, a surprising burst of energy that she hadn't felt in a long time. It made her feel powerful, no longer a victim. Taking action felt so much better than waiting to become roadside carnage. Grinning, she quickly leaned into the back seat, dug through her bags for her hiking boots and her raincoat. Within five minutes, she'd changed her shoes, zipped the ranch house key, her phone, the directions, and her wallet into the inside pocket of the coat, and chowed a granola bar.

Thunder rumbled just as she was reaching for the door handle. She hesitated for a split second, then looked around at the car. Another prison, just like her apartment.

Suddenly, she couldn't take another second of it. She had to be outside. She had to be moving. She had to be breathing in fresh air. *Now.*

So she shoved open the door, stepped into six inches of muddy, raging water, and got out. The wind hit hard, and the rain thundered down, and she realized it was really brutal out. She hesitated, one hand on the door frame, suddenly unsure what to do. What if it was longer than she thought to the ranch? What if she got lost? There was literally no one to come to aid. No cell service. No cars going past. But, there were coyotes, or at least one. They didn't attack people, though, she was pretty sure. *Crap.* Was she a total fool to get out of the car and start hiking? Or would she be a bigger fool to sit in her car until someone came past?

Probably hiking was the worse choice.

But dammit. She didn't want to sit around anymore. She wanted to move. To live. To feel her body work again.

Screw it.

She was hiking.

With a renewed sense of power, she slammed her door shut and headed up the embankment toward the highway. She made it halfway up the incline, then she felt her boots start to slide. She yelped, and fought for purchase, leaning down to brace her hands on the ground, but as she stood there, her feet slid all the way back down, she lost her grip and landed on her knees, and rode the muddy gravel all the way back down, landing with a sploosh in the muddy river that had trapped her car.

Noelle looked up at the ten-foot embankment of mud and gravel, and suddenly, she started to laugh. Oh, God. This was too insane. Her first day of replenishing her soul, and she was trapped by a hill of shale and mud? Energy rushed through her, a fire that made her entire body feel stronger than it had in years.

She backed up several steps, set her gaze on her goal, and then charged the hill. She made it halfway up again, and then her boots started to slide. She lunged forward, digging her hands into the mud as she fought to scramble up the side. She made it another few feet, sliding backwards almost as often as she made it forward.

Her breath was heaving in her chest, and she fought harder, her feet sliding down almost as fast as she was able to take a step forward. Rain poured over her, running down her neck and under her coat, and mud coated her hands to her wrists. Her jeans were soaked, there was cold mud oozing over the top of her boots, and her hair was glued to her cheeks by the mud and the rain. She was filthy, soaked, exhausted, and hadn't felt so alive in years. Grinning even as her fingernails were scraped by the gravel, she fought against gravity. Inch by inch, she scrambled higher, until she was almost at the top...and then her feet started to go again.

"Crap!" She lunged for the top of the embankment, and just missed it...and started to slide back down again–

A strong hand suddenly grabbed her wrist, jerking her to a stop mid-slide.

She looked up quickly to find a drenched, muddy cowboy in a long jacket, a dripping cowboy hat, and icy-blue eyes staring down at her, his fingers locked around her arm.

Noelle froze, shocked by the sight of him, by the way her belly leapt, by the sudden heat rushing through her body. Dear God, he was straight out of her teenage fantasies. A hot cowboy coming to her rescue?

No, not hot. Calling him hot was kind of like calling a wild, fully grown male mountain lion a cute little kitten. It was a supreme injustice to both the lion and the kitten. The man before her was pure, rugged male...the

34

kind of male that made her want to drop everything, sprint over to him, and surrender every aspect of herself to his raw masculinity.

There was something about the way he was standing there with his duster flapping in the heavy wind, his legs braced against the weight of her body, while the rain dripped off his hat that was just so primal. Delicious. Surreal. Hot. Like he was made of testosterone, Old West charm, and danger...with just a hint of cocky arrogance curving his mouth so seductively that a shiver went down her spine that had nothing to do with the fact she was soaking wet and closing in on hypothermia (yes, it was fifty degrees, but hypothermia wasn't choosy, was it?)

She couldn't quite believe how good it felt to stare at a man and notice how wide his shoulders were beneath his black jacket, or the way his quads bulged beneath his jean-clad thighs as he braced himself, as if his body was made for a life of outdoor roughness. She took a deep breath, wishing that he was close enough for her to catch a scent of him, a heady masculine scent that would make her stomach curl and her belly flutter like it had back when she used to feel alive. But all she could smell was the damp earth, the fresh rain, and the murkiness of the swampy river she'd just waded through...which was just as well. One more assault to her senses would likely send her romantically barren soul into testosterone-induced shock.

He lifted one eyebrow slowly, amusement flickering in his eyes, and suddenly, she realized she was gawking at him. Like, literally *gawking.* Heat flooded her cheeks, but she had nowhere to hide, nowhere else to look, not when it was his grip on her arm that was keeping her from tumbling back down the embankment to the muddy, bubbly water.

"Ready?" His voice rolled through her. Deep. Masculine. Rich. Her stomach literally vibrated in response.

"Ready? For what?" She had no idea what he was talking about. All she could think of was how kind and warm he sounded, a hint of gentleness in his voice that contrasted so sharply with the strapping strength of his frame, and the ease with which he was keeping her from sliding down the hill.

The amusement in his eyes deepened. "For me to haul you up here so you don't slide down again. Or I can let you go, if you prefer."

"Oh, right." She'd totally forgotten she was still standing at a forty-five-degree angle, several feet below him, on an embankment that was becoming increasingly unstable in the heavy rain. "Hauling me up would be fantastic, thanks."

He flashed her a grin so devastatingly charming that she forgot to breathe, and then he stepped back, using his body to counterbalance her as she scrambled up the last few feet and over the edge. She landed in front of him, her boots thudding on the even ground...and she realized that he was even more solid and tall when she was on his level than he'd looked when he was above her.

For a long moment, she didn't move, and neither did he. His hand was still locked around her arm, and she didn't pull away. They just stood there, the rain hammering down on them, sliding over her face, and down her neck.

She was close enough now to see the heavy whiskers on his face, a beard that he didn't quite allow to grow in. His jaw was hard and strong. His face angular. And his eyes...she forgot about everything else but his eyes. They were a deep, turbulent crystal blue that were so intense they literally took her breath away with the potency burning within them. She knew then that he wasn't simply a sinfully hot cowboy. He was more, something infinitely more complex, burdened by a weight so raw that he made her heart speed up. This man was *alive*, fermenting with power and passion that made her heart clench.

God, how long had it been since she'd felt alive like that?

His gaze traveled over her, across her face, over her muddy, soaking body, moving with a languid interest that made heat burn in her belly. His gaze flicked to her car, angled down in the ditch, and then back to her. "City girl?"

The way he said it didn't sound like an insult. It sounded like a seduction that made him promise to show her exactly how wild the cowboy life could be. She nodded. "Boston."

"Boston." He repeated the word, rolling it ever so slightly with a cowboy twang that made her belly tighten. "So, you must be Noelle Wilder." His gaze settled on her face. "I've been expecting you."

Chapter 5

YEAH, WYATT HAD been expecting a woman named Noelle Wilder from Boston, but he hadn't been expecting *her.* Not in any way.

When Bunny had told him she was doing a house swap for the next month so she could do some house hunting for her Cape Cod dream home, Wyatt had been annoyed. He didn't have time to babysit a city slicker, not when he had to figure out who the hell had doped his ride, and get his bull riding back on track, but he owed Bunny a lot, so he'd agreed.

He'd figured Noelle Wilder would be a pain in his ass. Afraid to get dirty. Needing shit from him he didn't have to give. Uptight. Maybe on the hunt for an affair with a cowboy that she could tell her friends about, showing up in high heels, makeup, and a need to seduce. He knew about those women. Hell, that was the only kind of woman who ever crossed his path.

Until now.

He hadn't expected the woman standing in front of him. Noelle was wearing jeans and hiking boots. She was soaking wet. Muddy from head to toe. Makeup-free. Rain was glistening on her cheeks, highlighting brown eyes so compelling he'd forgotten to breathe the moment he'd looked into them. She wasn't dressed to impress. She was dressed...for herself...and it had hit him straight in the gut the moment he'd walked to the top of the embankment and seen her struggling to climb it, refusing to succumb to gravity.

And she'd been laughing while she was doing it. *Laughing.*

She made him want to laugh, and he hadn't laughed in a long, damned time.

And now, she gazed up at him, her face glistening with rain. "You were expecting me?" she asked, repeating his words back to him. "Who are you?"

At the sound of her voice, something shifted inside Wyatt. There was such kindness in her voice, a warmth, a lack of pretense...a quiet, deep appreciation for the moment. He couldn't seem to tear his gaze off her face. "My name's Wyatt Parker. I'm the foreman on the Sleeping Bull Ranch. Bunny told me to keep an eye out for you."

"The foreman?" Noelle's eyes widened, and her gaze slipped off his face, checking him out with rapid, nervous interest.

His cock actually tightened at the feel of her gaze sweeping over him. His reaction shocked him. He was used to being checked out by women. The minute he had started having success as a bull rider, the women had flocked to him, wanting only a piece of his ass and his winnings. He'd learned fast and ugly not to trust anyone who looked at him that way, a lesson that Octavia had solidified when he'd thought she was an exception. He didn't even notice anymore when women checked him out...until now. Until Noelle's gaze brushed over him, a tentative, innocent exploration that ignited a fire in him that had been dormant for a long time.

Her gaze shot back to his face, and to his surprise, she pulled free of his grip, took several steps back and set her hands on her hips. She lifted her chin, and he literally felt the wall that she raised between them.

He narrowed his eyes, surprised by the way she tried to put distance between them. Women never did that, not with him. He didn't take it personally, because he knew that any bull rider with a halfway decent career got the same appreciation from women. Which made the fact that Noelle had stepped back a hell of a lot more interesting than if she had stepped forward.

He cocked his head, studying her. "Running the ranch for Bunny is just a part-time gig. I'm a bull rider." He never told anyone he was a bull rider, because he hated being judged by it. But he wanted to see what Noelle would do when she knew. Somehow, he needed to find out what she thought of that fact. "Last year's runner up at the finals." Today's tainted sideliner.

To his satisfaction, Noelle didn't inch forward. She didn't get a flash of interest in her eyes. There was no hint of greed in her face. In fact, her forehead wrinkled. "Can't you die from that?"

Her question made him tense, because, you know, he'd almost died two months ago. "Yes."

It was only because he was watching her so closely that he saw her flinch. It wasn't a superficial, dramatic response designed to stroke his ego about how manly he was. There was a genuine flash of fear and anguish in her eyes, and she physically recoiled, folding her arms across her chest. "I don't understand that," she said. "I don't understand how you could do something that could kill you. Don't you realize what a gift it is to be alive?"

Her voice was almost desperate, edged with a grief that struck him right in his gut. He swore under his breath, and knew then that someone she loved had died on her. Someone who mattered to her. Someone whose death had changed her view of life forever. Suddenly, he saw her differently. He saw the shadows in her eyes, the hollowness of her cheeks, the way she hugged herself, as if she had to hold herself up. He understood why she was taking a month off from her life to hang out on some Oregon ranch. "Who died?" he asked softly.

Shock flashed across her face, and for a second, he thought she wouldn't answer. But she did. "My husband. A year ago. He was sick for three years."

Her voice was tight, guarded, and exhausted. He knew it had been a long three years, and a long year since. "I'm sorry." Protectiveness surged through him, a deep, instinctive need to surround her with his strength, to protect her from the grief trying to hold onto her, to make it safe for her to breathe again.

She nodded. "Thanks." She managed a smile. "But we have to keep living, right? Otherwise it's an insult to those who die young."

He thought of his dad and nodded. "Agreed." Suddenly, he didn't resent Bunny's request to make sure Noelle was safe. He accepted it. He embraced it. In fact, to his surprise, a small part of him actually regretted that he would be leaving the ranch in a few days to compete.

The moment he had that thought, he swore under his breath. He'd already given up everything for a woman once, and he had learned his lesson. God, how he had learned his lesson. He'd known Noelle about sixty seconds, and he was already regretting leaving her? What the hell? He was going to ride this weekend, and nothing was going to keep him home. Not even this woman from Boston, who looked like the weight of life was going to crush her.

He cleared his throat, resisting the urge to close the distance between them and draw her into a hug, to somehow support her. He would make sure she was safe, yeah, but that was it. He wasn't going to step over that line that he'd sworn never to be dragged across again. "Tell you what," he said. "I'll ride back to the ranch, get a tractor, and come back and pull your car out." He liked that plan. It helped and protected her, but put some distance between them, and that powerful-as-hell tug between them.

She glanced past his shoulder, and he saw her eyes widen when she saw his horse. "You rode out here?"

"Yeah. I was checking fences." He saw her shiver, and he swore, suddenly aware of the pounding rain hammering them both. Her face was streaked with rain, her jeans sodden against her legs, her raincoat no longer beading with rain because it had maxed out its capacity to keep her dry. He frowned. "You should get back in your car and get dry. I'll be back in about an hour." If he rode hard, he could make it home in forty-five minutes. It was pushing it, but he wasn't leaving her out here any longer than he had to.

She blinked, drawing his attention to the raindrops clumping at the ends of her eyelashes. "You want to leave me here?" The question was careful, as if she wasn't sure how that made her feel.

"I don't want to leave you, specifically. I want to help you, but I need to get a tractor to get your car out." He cleared his throat, resisting the urge to throw her on the back of his horse and haul her up against him. "I'll be back as soon as I can."

She looked over her shoulder at the car, and then back at his horse. He saw the flash of fear in her eyes, and he swore. He knew then that she didn't want to wait there. "You'll be safe in the car. Dry. You can turn on the heat." He didn't want her out in the rain on his horse...but at the same time, some part of him didn't want to leave her behind.

Yeah, she would be safe there. Nothing was going to happen. They were already on the ranch property, and no one would be coming by. But hell...it didn't feel right to leave her.

She looked at the horse again, and then back at him. "I'd rather ride with you."

His gut clenched, and he had a sudden image of her riding in front of him on Lightning, leaning back against him while he held her securely in front of him. At the thought of her nestled between his thighs, his gut tightened with the surge of lust he hadn't felt in too damn long. *Shit.* He didn't have time for this, for a woman, for reacting this way. For hell's sake, he had a possible murderer hunting him, and a bull riding career to resurrect in three days. He did not have time to notice her like this. But he couldn't help it. He just couldn't stop staring into her eyes, from wanting to chase away the shadows haunting her, from needing to protect her...

No. He had to keep his distance. He had too much going on. She had to stay in her car, not park herself on his lap for a longer ride in the rain. No way. He opened his mouth to tell her that, but the words that came out weren't what he'd intended. "You want to ride with me?"

The moment he asked the question, he regretted it...and knew it was the only thing he wanted to ask. It might not make sense for a shitload of reasons, but there was nothing more he wanted in that moment than to have his thighs on either side of hers, his arm around her waist, anchoring her back against his chest, his coat tucked around her to keep her protected from the storm. He wanted her where he could make sure she was safe, and the only place that fit that bill right now, was on the back of his horse in his arms.

Relief flashed over her face. "I don't want to be in the car." Her voice was quiet, almost a whisper, but he still heard the desperation. "I would love to ride with you."

His gut shifted at her word choice. *I would love to ride with you.* Shit. He liked that. He liked that she had no doubt, that she trusted him completely, even though he was a stranger. She was right to trust him. There was no way in hell he'd hurt her. If he took her with him, her safety would be completely dependent on him. *Completely.* Damn. He liked that. No, he didn't like it. He *loved* it. He stood taller, and whistled low under his breath. His mount, Lightning, trotted over, and stopped beside him. Wyatt gathered the reins, and then held out his hand to her.

For a long moment, she didn't move, and he tensed. Was she going to retreat to her car? Decide she was safer in a ditch in her car than on a horse with him? Logic said she was, but something primal deep inside him resisted. "I'll keep you safe," he said quietly.

Her gaze flicked to his, and he didn't miss the flash of yearning in her eyes, coupled with a vulnerability that made his chest tighten. He knew then that no one ever kept her safe. No one ever took care of her. She took care of herself, and the people around her.

He wanted to give her that gift. He wanted it to be him who gave her even a few minutes of feeling like she didn't have to fight her battles herself...or at least this battle, for the next hour. He flicked his fingers, beckoning her toward him. "Come on, Noelle. Ride with me."

She took a deep breath, and she lifted her chin.

He knew then, before she spoke, before she moved, that she was going to say yes. Anticipation roared through him, a fierce, roaring sensation of rightness as she slowly lifted her hand.

His entire body hummed in anticipation as he waited for her to set her hand in his, but the moment he felt her fingers in his, peace settled deep inside him, all the way to his core, and he knew that this woman had come into his life for a reason, and he was going to find out what it was.

Chapter 6

T HE MOMENT NOELLE set her hand in Wyatt's, she felt like her world had come to a crashing stop, hovering in suspended abeyance, every one of her senses completely focused on him. His hand was warm, a stark contrast to her frozen fingers. He didn't seem to notice or care how muddy her hands were after her climb up the embankment. Instead of pulling away, his fingers closed around hers, cradling her hand in his.

Her heart seemed to stutter, and heat poured through her, starting in her chest and radiating through her belly and down her arms. Dear God. She wanted him. Not just an attraction, but something deep inside her soul was calling out for him, to him, needing his touch, his kindness...him.

Suddenly terrified, she jerked her hand back and folded her arms over her chest, trying to fight off the longing coursing through her. Her heart ached, and she was suddenly filled with the most haunting sense of loss and emotion, tearing through the shields she had erected so carefully over the last four years, making herself numb enough to handle everything. Suddenly, emotions swelled over her, a flood of every emotion she'd held at bay for so long, all of them triggered by the simple touch of Wyatt's hand.

Tears flooded her eyes, and her breath became labored as she fought to hold herself together. She saw the surprise on his face, and she instinctively turned away, hugging herself as she stumbled back toward the embankment. "I think I'll wait in the car," she managed to croak out. Dear God. What was wrong with her? She couldn't even breathe. Couldn't think. Couldn't talk. There were so many images flashing through her mind. The moment when she found out David was dying. The moment when she'd realized that she would have to live life without him. That sense of loss and loneliness. The need to be loved and supported that she'd crushed so ruthlessly when she'd realized she had to be the strong one. Anger. Loss. Loneliness. Betrayal. And need. God, the *need* was almost overwhelming. A need to be held, to be loved, to be supported, to be understood, to be nurtured, to be accepted exactly as she was.

Somehow, some way, for some reason, Wyatt had unlocked everything inside her that made her human, that made her feel, that made her unable to hide the depth of her need for connection...all of them luxuries she couldn't afford, emotions that made her vulnerable, feelings that terrified her.

She didn't want to feel them. She didn't want to acknowledge how badly she wanted to be more than what she was. She couldn't face how badly she needed her life to be more than she had allowed it to be. She had to become numb again. *She had to.*

She reached the embankment and stumbled over the

edge, her feet sliding as she lost her balance. She was vaguely aware of Wyatt calling her name, but she didn't stop. She couldn't stop. The tears were too heavy, and gravity was too strong, dragging her down the embankment in a rush of mud and sliding shale...

Her feet suddenly slipped out from under her, and she yelped as she fell backward–

Right into Wyatt.

His arms snapped around her waist, catching her against him as they slid down the embankment together, the rocks and shale tumbling down into the rising water. They landed with a splash in the water, with her trapped against his chest as they fell backward, with her landing in his lap.

The heat from his body tore through her, and the strength of his frame surrounding her, like a solid shield protecting her, nurturing her, keeping her safe. She knew she had to get up. She knew it was ridiculous to be sitting on the lap of some man she didn't know, but she couldn't make herself move. She just froze, her eyes closed, her fingers wrapped around his forearms. She was trapped by the feel of his body encircling hers, by his warmth penetrating the cold that seemed to go so deeply inside her, by the steady thud of his heart against her back.

The water lapped over their feet, a rhythmic cold undulation over her boots, and rain hammered them, but still, she couldn't move. She felt like she was cocooned in a surreal moment, an oasis in a hurricane where the wind and rain and cold couldn't touch her.

Wyatt shifted, and she felt him lean forward until his face was next to hers, his chin almost resting on her shoulder. "What happened up there?" he asked.

She closed her eyes, gripping his forearms even harder. With him behind her, she couldn't see him. It was as if his strength, the feel of his body against hers was a fantasy she could lose herself in, not a real man that she had to deal with.

"Noelle?" His voice was warm and deep, wrapping around her like a blanket enveloping her heart. "What did I do to spook you like that?"

"I'm sorry," she whispered. "I just...I'll just wait in the car."

He laughed softly, a laugh that felt like a warm caress. "Sweetheart, as heartless as I may be, there's no chance I'm going to leave you behind when you're in tears, drenched, and trapped by a river that's rising faster than I like. When I said you could stay behind earlier, I didn't realize how fast the water was rising. I'm happy to sit here until you're ready to go, but leaving you behind stopped being a possibility when I saw your face after I touched your hand. The fact that the water's rising fast seals the deal."

Noelle scrunched her eyes shut even more tightly, as if closing her eyes could somehow protect her from the kindness he was wrapping around her, that he was making her crave so badly. "I know how to swim. I'll be fine."

He laughed again, drawing a tiny smile from her, because he'd noticed and caught her attempt at humor. "Because swimming upriver in a storm-surge stream is definitely a good plan." His arms tightened around her waist. "I don't mind waiting until you're ready. I've always wanted to sit on this particular embankment during a storm, but I'm always so damn busy I never take the time, so this is all good." He stretched his legs out on either side of hers, as if he were on a tropical beach enjoying the sun. "Nothing like taking time to enjoy life, right?"

This time, she was the one who laughed, a tiny, heart-wrenching laugh that forced the tiniest crack in the emotions threatening to overwhelm her. "The rain is lovely," she agreed. "I especially like how it mixes with the mud as it runs down my neck and under my coat."

"I know. That icy chill is the stuff of fantasies. And getting my ass frozen by cold mud is a damn gift. I can't think of a better place to hang out." As he spoke, the mud gave way, and they both slid a few more feet down into the water.

Wyatt dug his heels in, stopping their descent. Noelle could feel the muscles in his thighs flexing as he braced them, and her heart did a little flip. He was pure strength, rugged, outdoorsy strength, not a man who had already given up on life. So different than what she had lived with for so long.

Noelle opened her eyes and looked at her rental car, askew in the rising water. The water was halfway up the tires, and she could see that it was still rising. "How high is the water going to get?"

"I don't know. It's a hell of a storm coming in." Wyatt's arms were tight around her waist, and he sounded relaxed, as if he could truly spend the next couple hours sitting behind her, holding her, keeping her from sliding the rest of the way into the water.

Noelle sighed. "You're really going to sit here with me until I'm ready to go, aren't you?"

"Yes, ma'am."

"Why?"

He was silent for a moment, and she felt his arm tighten around her waist again. Finally, he spoke. "You want the answer I'd give most people, or the truth?"

From the way he asked the question, she knew the truth was going to be raw and uncensored, a gritty truth that she wasn't prepared to handle. She wanted to be hard and numb again, not open the door to anything that would keep her from pulling herself together. He was a stranger. She didn't want raw and gritty from him, and she didn't know why he'd even offered it.

But as she sat there, tears still mixing with the rain on her cheeks, her heart still aching, her body cold and numb, suddenly she didn't want numb and emotionless anymore. She wanted to feel something. To be forced to feel. To be given the freedom to shiver, cry, yearn, and ache. "Truth," she whispered.

He leaned forward, his breath warm against the side of her neck. "I would sit here for hours until you're ready to get up for one reason."

She looked down at her hands still wrapped around his forearms. "What's that reason?"

"Because you make me want to."

Tears filled her eyes again, but this time, they weren't tears of grief. They were tears of... God. She didn't even know. "Why?"

He sighed. "Because life broke something inside you, and I have never needed anything in my life as much as I need to fix it."

Broken. His words settled inside her. Broken? Was she broken? She closed her eyes. "I didn't feel broken until you took my hand. I thought I was fine."

"We're all like that, until we hit that landmine that blows apart all our pretenses and shields."

Noelle stared at the muddy water bubbling past her. His words made sense. They made her feel normal, as if it was okay for her soul to be broken into so many pieces that it felt like they would never fit together again. She took a deep breath. "Thank you for saying that."

"You're welcome." He fell silent, and the only sound was the storm. The rain hammering on her car. The rush of the water. The roar of the wind. The sound of rain pelting her coat...

And the sound of his breath, steady and even, waiting.

Noelle took a deep breath, and she felt her emotions begin to settle. Her muscles began to loosen, and the tightness in her chest eased. She became aware of his body still framing hers, protective but not overpowering. She glanced at her hands, still tightly gripping his forearms. Why did she want to hold onto him so much? And why did he want to sit here with her? He answered the question, but only partially.

"When I was growing up, Bunny used to tell me that if you tell your sorrows to the rain, it will wash them out of your heart."

"Really? Did it work?"

"I can't remember. I don't think I ever did it. I considered myself too much of a badass to have sorrows, let alone talk about them." There was humor in his voice, a self-deprecating awareness that made Noelle smile.

She lifted her face to the rain, and let it wash over her cheeks. It was cold, but it was also fresh and cleansing. She closed her eyes, feeling each droplet hit her eyelashes. Sorrow and sadness seemed to well up inside her, a grief that wanted to reach out to the rain coming down. She had so much to say to the rain, that she had no words. So she just sat there, letting it wash over her face, until the shivers from the cold penetrated so deeply that she couldn't stop shaking.

Wyatt sighed. "Time to go, Noelle. It's too cold out here. I can feel you trembling."

She didn't want to get up. She didn't want to go with him. She didn't want to stop shivering, because the cold took all her attention, making it impossible to think about David, or about how good it felt to be in Wyatt's arms. But his words made her aware of how badly she was trembling, of how cold she felt deep inside, as if she had finally found the darkest place inside her and unlocked it.

She didn't know why this moment, why this man,

why this rain had unlocked the shields she held around her heart, but it had. It hurt. God, it hurt. But at the same time, it felt like the weight of a thousand lifetimes was suddenly lifting from her chest, allowing her to breathe.

She suddenly realized that she wanted to breathe again, truly breathe, no matter how much it hurt to do so.

Wyatt shifted behind her, and she felt him stand up. Deprived of the warmth of his body, cold air rushed across her back, and she suddenly felt a thousand times colder. But just as quickly, he moved in front of her, standing calf deep in the river. His icy blue eyes settled on her face, and her heart seemed to stutter in her chest.

God, she'd forgotten how intense her reaction to him was.

He held out his hands to her. "Let's go."

He didn't give her a choice...and that felt good. She was too tired to make any decisions, to decide when she'd had enough, to be ready to ride with him. She'd been the one making every single decision, even the heart-wrenchingly difficult ones, for the last four years, and it felt good to have someone make one for her, just this time, just this moment. "Okay."

He cocked an eyebrow. "Do I dare take your hand again?"

She laughed, a laugh that felt rusty and good at the same time. "We can try." She set her hands in his. The moment her palms touched his, heat rushed through her, but this time, it didn't feel scary. Maybe it was because he'd sat in the mud with her. Maybe it was because she was too cold to be scared. Maybe it was because the rain had indeed washed away some of her pain. It didn't matter. She just knew that she felt better, and it was because of him.

His eyebrows went up, and then he grinned. "You're still facing me. That's a fantastic start." He gripped her hand tightly. "Let's go, sweetheart. Shelter is calling us." He started up the embankment, his grip strong and firm, his body angled to give her leverage as he used his body as her anchor to follow him up.

Noelle hesitated for only a brief moment, glancing back at her car. Somehow, she knew that once she went up that embankment with him, there was no going back. He was too real, and her reaction to him was too intense. She'd told Kate no complications, and Wyatt was all about complications...but she wanted them. She wanted them with every fiber of her rain-drenched soul.

He paused and looked back at her, his grip still tight on her hand. "Coming?"

She studied him for a long moment. His intense blue eyes. The shadows in his eyes. The warmth in his expression. He was strong and solid, but at the same time, she saw the sorrow in his eyes, and realized suddenly that he needed someone to lean on, just like she did. He'd needed to sit there on that embankment as much as she did. Wyatt was strength, but there was also something broken inside him, something that he needed her to fix.

She relaxed. That was something she knew how to handle: being strong for someone else. She could to do this. Yes, her reaction to him was strong, but she could handle it. She'd been meant to find him, and she knew then that they were meant to help each other. Team healing. Not love. Not lust. Not romance.

She'd come out here to find herself, not fall in love with a cowboy. So what if he was tempting? So what if her heart felt melty? She'd fallen in love once, and it had nearly destroyed her.

Not again.

Not even with him.

He raised his brows. "Noelle?"

She took a deep breath. Go with him, but keep a distance? Yes. She could do that. She had to do it. *She could do this.* "Yes, I'm coming. Let's go."

Chapter 7

THEY REACHED THE top of the embankment, and Wyatt didn't let go of her hand even after they were both on solid ground. He turned to face her as she summited, watching her as she reached him. He straightened up, and she realized he was taller than she'd noticed before. She came up to the middle of his chest, and his shoulders were so wide she felt tiny in comparison.

Rightness surged through her, that same rightness as when she'd felt the strength of his quads on either side of her hips. She was startled by how good it felt not to have to be the strong one, the one trying to hold everything together. He gave off the aura of strength and power, and it felt incredible...but even as she thought it, guilt flashed through her. Guilt that she was appreciating his strength, as if it was an insult to David.

She didn't want to compare them. She didn't want David to be less in her memories, just because Wyatt was strong. She wanted to simply appreciate this moment, and not let it get tangled up in all the noise in her head.

"What's wrong?" Wyatt didn't move away, his gaze focused on hers.

"I just–" She stopped. What was she going to say? That she was in love with the fact he was strong and rugged? Because that would sound sane and reasonable, right? Not.

He cocked an eyebrow, studying her as if she was a great enigma he was getting increasingly interested in figuring out.

Heat rushed through her, and instinctively, unable to stop herself, she put her hand on his chest over his heart. He didn't move away, and after a moment, she could feel the steady thump of his heart, strong and solid. Her fingers dug into his chest, as if she could grab onto his life force and hold it in her hand. "You're just so alive," she whispered. "I forgot what that was like." She splayed her fingers, feeling the strength of his muscles where she was used to feeling paper-thin flesh barely stretched over bony ribs. "It's like nothing could ever stop you. It's... amazing." She couldn't keep the wonder out of her voice, and she couldn't make herself break contact.

It just felt so good to be touching a man who was so alive. It made her feel like there was electricity leaping off him into her body, igniting her with strength instead of draining it.

For a long moment, Wyatt didn't react, and they both stood there in the pouring rain, the heat from his body searing her cold palm. She could feel the ripple of his muscles beneath her hand, the movement of his chest as he breathed. How many times had she sat with her hand on David's chest, checking to see if he was only sleeping, or if he was finally gone?

With Wyatt, it was so different. He exuded raw

strength and power, a man who seemed like he would never be bested by frailty or disease. Her hand started to tremble, maybe with cold, maybe with the sheer exhaustion of trying to hold onto everything for so long, and knowing that there was suddenly this great strength in front of her, a man who could do things like catch her when she stumbled, even down a slick, muddy embankment.

She looked up at him, and she was startled to see him watching her intently. His head was ducked slightly, as if he were using the brim of his hat to shield her from the rain and even the world. His eyes were inscrutable, and his mouth was in a tight line, but she didn't feel like he was angry. Just intense. Just...God. He was just raw, untamed male, wasn't he? Desire raced through her, a longing to feel his arms around her, to lose herself in the strength of his body, to let him take her away from the memories she couldn't escape.

His gaze dropped to her mouth, and she swallowed, her heart hammering in her chest as she felt the heat from his stare. Dear God, he wasn't going to kiss her, was he? That would be so absurd. She didn't even know him, and...she suddenly became aware of how hot her palm was. Her gaze went to his chest, to her pale hand spread across his chest, and gradual, horrifying awareness flooded her. She was *fondling* a complete stranger in the middle of nowhere...but at the same time, he didn't feel like a stranger. She felt safe with him. Secure. Protected. Like he'd touched a piece of her heart simply by being himself...which made no sense, right?

What was *wrong* with her? Embarrassment flooded her cheeks and she jerked her hand back. "I'm so sorry. I didn't mean to touch you like that. I mean, I don't even know you or–"

He touched his index finger to her lips, silencing her.

He shook his head once. "It's okay." Just two simple words were all he said before he moved past her to retrieve his horse. Two simple words muttered in a deep baritone was all he'd offered her, but they rolled through her like a seductive caress that made all the tension and embarrassment disappear.

She took a deep breath, trying to gather herself even as she was unable to tear her gaze from him as he turned toward his horse, murmuring softly to the animal. She caught the name Lightning as Wyatt ran his hand gently over the velvet nose of his horse. Lightning ducked his head, pressing his face against Wyatt's chest, and he bowed his head, murmuring softly to the animal.

Her heart turned over at the moment of intimacy between man and horse, at the trust that so clearly bonded them together. The simple, beautiful connection touched her, and she had to turn her head away to fight off the tears.

God, she wanted a moment like that. A moment with Wyatt bending his head toward hers, holding her quietly, silently promising that he would always look out for her, offering her the strength he carried with him so effortlessly. Not because she was weak, because she wasn't, and she knew that. Not because she needed a man, because she knew she didn't. But because there was nothing as beautiful as that feeling of safety in the arms of someone else who would never, ever walk away if you needed them.

"Noelle?"

Wyatt's deep voice pulled her attention back to him. He was running his palm over Lightning's nose as he watched her. "Have you ridden before?" he asked, mercifully changing the subject to a neutral one, prying her attention away from her thoughts before she could do something absurd like beg him to pat her nose like he was patting his horse's.

Relieved, she nodded. "I rode English as a kid," she said. "I know how to stay on." She glanced at the horse, who had turned his shaggy head to look at her. "Never Western, though."

"Same concept," he said. "Want a leg up?"

Heat flooded her at his suggestion of giving her a boost onto the horse. She wasn't sure she trusted herself to touch him. She glanced desperately at the stirrup, but it was too high. There was no way she would be able to get her foot up there, despite bi-weekly excursions to the yoga studio for a month, two years ago. Who knew that kind of investment wouldn't pay off years later? "Yes, okay."

He grunted his acquiescence and moved beside her. "On three."

"On three." She grasped the saddle and bent her left leg at the knee. His hands closed around her lower leg, just beneath her knee. God, oh, *God*, it felt good to feel his hands on her. It was even more intense than when she'd touched him, because it had been so long since she'd *been* touched by someone else, by a man, one she was attracted to, who made her feel like a woman, soft, vulnerable, and desirable. She closed her eyes, fighting the sudden surge of emotions through her.

"Ready?" he asked.

Ready? To squeeze onto that saddle with him, when the mere touch of his hands on her leg was so overwhelming? No, she wasn't ready. She would never be ready. "Ready." Her voice was shaky, and she hoped that he attributed it to the fact that she was shivering violently from the cold.

"On three." He tightened his grip on her leg. "One. Two. Three." On three, he boosted her up at the same time that she pushed off. He lifted her easily onto Lightning's back, and she sank down into the deep saddle. The drenched leather sent an icy chill through her jeans almost immediately, but Wyatt swung up behind her before she had time to get cold. His pelvis was up against her butt, and his chaps were cold and wet against the backs of her thighs. As he reached around her to take the reins, she felt like she was being cocooned by his strength, and dammit, it felt too good...the kind of good that she wanted to hold onto forever.

She hadn't had a moment she'd wanted to last forever in a very long time, and it felt amazing.

"Lean back against me," he said, his voice gruff.

She stiffened against her urge to do exactly that. "Um, no, I'm all set–"

"You're not all set. You're shivering. You need protection from the rain."

"Oh..." She suddenly became aware of the rain hammering at her even more fiercely than before. Her teeth were actually chattering now. Silently, refusing to be stupid, she leaned back against him.

His arm went around her belly and he pulled her back against him, cutting off all space between them. "Good?" he asked.

"Yes, great, thanks." It felt so surreal to be held in his arms, to have him taking care of her. It felt so good, too good, so overwhelming that she wanted to cry. But she didn't want to be anywhere else.

Chapter 8

WYATT NUDGED HIS horse into a trot, grimacing when the gentle movement of his
mount made Noelle rock against him, in a
rhythm that was all too tempting. He shifted, trying to
pull his hips back, but there was nowhere to go.

He swore, trying not to think about the fact that his
arm was just beneath her breasts. Yeah, his forearm
might be only millimeters from contact with them, but it
was a chasm he wasn't going to cross. What the hell was
he doing even thinking about them? He'd seen her tears.
He'd seen the loss in her eyes when she'd marveled over
the fact he was alive. So what if his entire body had gone
into overdrive when she'd touched him? That was no ex-
cuse.

She needed someone to rescue her, to help her, not to
grope her.

And hell, he had sworn off women the day he'd found
out the truth about his ex-fiancée.

And yet, despite both facts, he couldn't stop thinking about how Noelle felt against his chest. He couldn't help but notice the faint scent of flowers that seemed to cling to her. He couldn't help but wrap his jacket more snugly around her, and pull her more tightly against him, so that he could use his body and his jacket to ease the shivers wracking her body.

He had to hold her close, but damn, he didn't have to notice it. He cleared his throat. "So, um, Noelle, what do you do for work?" The moment he asked the question, he grimaced. Work? He'd asked about work? A woman so appealing that she'd taken his breath away with one look of her eyes was in his arms, and he'd asked her about *work*?

But even as he thought it, he felt her relax slightly, as if she, too, was in need of something to take her mind off the intimacy of their position. "I'm a writer. A mystery novelist."

His eyebrows shot up. "Seriously? That's cool as shit."

She laughed softly, relaxing even more against him. "Yes, except I can't think of an idea for my next book. It's been almost a year since it was due, but my brain stopped working."

He didn't need to ask why she'd had writer's block. He could figure it out. "Kind of like how I lost the ability to ride bulls. It's something you've done your whole life, and suddenly, your ability to do it just vanishes."

She looked over her shoulder at him, surprise on her face. "You forgot how to ride bulls?"

Shit. He didn't want to be thinking about the shit-storm of his professional life right now. Grimacing, he shrugged. "Reentry issues. No biggie."

She kept looking at him, and he knew suddenly that she saw so much more than he wanted her to see. So much more than he wanted to see himself. "What happened?" she asked.

He swore again, "Nothing–" But he cut himself off as he spoke, stopped by the expression on her face. She wanted to know. She was struggling, and she needed to connect, to know she wasn't the only one. Swearing, he ground his jaw. "I took a bad crash a couple months ago. The bull was..." He thought of Jesse's visit earlier in the day and swore. "You'd like this, mystery girl. Turns out my bull was drugged, apparently to try to kill me. They suspended me because they thought I'd juiced my ride. Earlier today, they decided that since it was attempted murder, I'm not such a bad guy, and they lifted my suspension. So, I get to ride this weekend, if I can get my damn seat back–"

He stopped as she twisted all the way around, almost sideways on his horse so she could look at him. "Someone tried to *murder* you?"

"Apparently."

Interest gleamed in her eyes, a spark of light that made something tighten in his gut. "That's so cool. Who do you think it was?"

"Cool?" He stared at her. "You think it's cool?"

Heat flushed her cheeks. "Well, I mean, I don't think it's cool on a personal level, but I write mysteries. I've never met anyone in real life who has been almost murdered. What was it like? Were you scared? Is it creepy? Are you always looking over your shoulder now? What if they try again this weekend?"

There was so much excitement in her voice that Wyatt couldn't help but laugh. Suddenly, his stress about the bull riding and Jesse's visit dissipated, chased away by her excitement. "This is *my* potential murder that you find so entertaining. You realize that, don't you?" Somehow, saying it to her took away some of the weight that had been crushing him.

She nodded. "Totally. Do you know who it is? Any ideas?"

He raised his brows. "My friend Brody thinks it's my ex-fiancée, but I don't see her turning to murder."

"Oh...I bet that's weird to have to think about who might want to murder you." She eyed him. "Do you want help? I am an expert on murder, in that 'totally imaginary, far-removed-from-reality' kind of way."

A part of him was tempted to say yes, but he quickly dismissed that thought when he considered the fact that it was actual murder they were talking about. "Thanks, but I don't think getting involved with the potential murderer is exactly what Bunny had in mind when she did the house swap with you. Jesse Knight is an investigator who works for the tour, and he's working on it. If anyone can figure out who it is, it's him."

Even as he spoke, he saw the excitement in Noelle's eyes fade, and he felt her energy sag. Before he could even think about it, he added, "but I'm happy to fill you in, in case you think of something that we don't."

When her face lit up again, he knew why he'd said it. The look on her face was the only reward he needed. He had no idea why he felt so compelled to reach out and try to help this woman, but he did. He had learned long ago not to question his instincts. With Octavia, he had ignored his reservations, and he'd paid the price. With Noelle, there were no reservations. Every instinct was honed in on his need to protect her, to help her, and to wipe away the shadows still clinging to her, so that's what he was doing. At this point, he was too damn bitter and cynical to do anything except follow his gut, and his gut was telling him to take care of Noelle, end of story.

If letting her brainstorm who might've drugged that bull ignited that spirit that she had come here to find, then he was okay with that. He was going to make damn sure she stayed out of danger, but what harm could a little brainstorming cause?

She grinned at him, and he could almost feel her mind cranking into gear, as if years of dust and rust were being shed. "Tell me why you think your ex-fiancée might have tried to kill you. I mean, there are bad breakups and all, but murder seems a little extreme."

Wyatt glanced past her, checking how far they still had to ride. They were nearing the ranch, but they still had a few minutes. He was going to take them straight to the barn, because taking care of his horse was his number one priority, as it would be with any half-decent cowboy. He took a deep breath, gritting his teeth as he thought back to that moment a year ago, when his life had changed, when he had finally stopped believing in anything good.

He shifted his position in the saddle, and Noelle nestled more securely against him. Her body was relaxed, and moving in sync with him, and he liked it. It felt right. He sighed, focusing on the feel of her body against his as he began to speak. "I met Octavia a few years ago. She was working for the tour in the public relations department, so she was at all the events. She seemed cool, not obsessed with the bull riders, like a lot of the women are."

He heard Noelle chuckle. "You guys are considered hotties out there, huh?"

He laughed softly. "Yeah, I guess." There'd been a time when that had felt good, to be treated like he mattered. "My dad was a piece of shit, and he got kicked off the tour for cheating. It took a while to get anyone to see me as anyone but the son of a cheater. Octavia was on my side, and she did a piece on me that changed everything for me. She made me look good, and stood by me, saying I wasn't my old man."

He remembered the day that article had come out. It had blown his mind to see those kinds of words written about him, after all the shit he'd lived with his whole life. "My dad thought I was shit, and I spent my life trying to become good enough to impress him. Bull riding was all he knew, so that was how I planned to do it. I was young and stupid then, thinking that my dad's approval actually mattered, so when Octavia published that article, it paved the way for people on the tour to give me a chance. It felt damn good, really damn good...too good. It made me feel indebted to her, in a way that I should have been too smart to succumb to."

Noelle relaxed against Wyatt as she listened to him. She could hear the edge to his voice, showing her the complexity of his relationship with his father. She felt a slight tinge of jealousy as he spoke about Octavia being the first to believe in him, a surprising emotion, given that she'd just met him.

"No one had ever seen me the way Octavia presented me in her article. Because of her, I became the rising star of the tour, a rookie who had the potential to be the best. I became pretty arrogant, convinced that I ruled the world." He ground his jaw, thinking back to that period of his life, when he was so caught up in the glam and the glory. "I became a complete ass, I got sucked up into all the glamour and glitz, just the way my dad had, so long ago. At the start of my second season, I proposed to Octavia, and she said yes. I thought I had it all. I thought that I'd figured out what mattered."

Noelle glanced over her shoulder, surprised by his comment that he'd become like his dad. "Did you cheat like he did?" Even as she asked the question, she knew the answer. There was no way the man with his arms around her had a dishonest bone in his body. Her soul knew it, without question.

"No, but it was close." His body tensed, and Noelle knew that he was about to get to the nitty-gritty, to the ugly part. "I made the finals of the tour that year. I was the front-runner to win the championship. On the night before the last day of the finals, I was tied for first with two rounds to ride the next night. I was feeling good, and I knew I had a chance to win. Octavia..." He paused, and she felt his arms tighten around her waist. "Octavia came to my hotel room that night. She said she had a chance for us to earn a shit ton of money. She said the odds were in my favor to win, but if I got bucked off the bull, we could both earn two hundred grand."

Noelle stiffened, startled. "She wanted you to throw the finals? After all you had worked to accomplish?"

Wyatt felt the hardness settle in his gut, just like it had that moment when he stared at Octavia, realization dawning. "Yeah, she did. Turns out, she was also shacking up with the bull rider who was tied for first. He wanted to win, and he agreed to split his winnings if I pulled my ride. He got a couple bookies to chip in, and it was set up to be a big payout. Apparently..." The bile churned in his throat, that same sick feeling of betrayal. "Apparently, she made the same offer to the rider in second, who she was also sleeping with. Both of us get bucked off, and her number one wins. She was planning to take out half a million between all the deals. Half a damned million."

Noelle felt sick to her stomach at his words. How could anyone betray someone like that, someone they loved, someone who loved them? "I'm so sorry, Wyatt. What did you do?"

"I turned her in. She lost her job. The other two bull riders denied knowing anything about her plan, so they were cleared. People accused me of making up shit to try to get them kicked off. It got ugly, and we all got bucked off in the final round, and someone else won. Octavia got another job on the tour, but she hates me now, as do the other two bull riders involved, both of whom said I initiated it. Nothing was proven, so we were all cleared, but it got us labeled."

Noelle bit her lip, feeling the tension in Wyatt's body as he spoke. "She betrayed you," she said softly. "She said she loved you, and then betrayed you. That's the worst kind of betrayal."

"Yeah." Wyatt took a deep breath, feeling the way Noelle settled more deeply against him. She didn't pull away, she didn't judge him for being so stupid. She just wrapped her hand around his wrist, an unspoken gesture of support. Something inside him tightened, something deeper than he'd felt in a long time. "Octavia turned on me, not the others. She told everyone it was my idea, and that I'd turned her in after I chickened out. She had no proof, but the seed was planted, especially given my dad. So, yeah, since then, there's an invisible asterisk next to every single ride I take."

And now, thanks to that cursed ride two months ago, there would never be any doubt in anyone's mind that he was a cheater. "Even though I was cleared of that bull ride a couple months ago, the damage is done. Everything I do will be dirty." And he hated that, hated that more than anything. "That's why I'm riding this weekend. I'm not going to walk away and let those bastards take riding away from me." He heard the anger in his voice, and he hated it. He hated that he was pissed, that he let them get to him, but he couldn't stop it.

Noelle was silent for a moment, and the only sound was the hammering of the rain, and the sound of his horse's feet sloshing through the muddy puddles. Then she spoke. "Did your dad really cheat?"

"Yeah. I asked him just before he died. He did." He'd finally posed that question a year ago, when he'd been set up by Octavia. He'd finally realized that maybe his dad's claims of innocence all thosee years had been true. He'd realized that maybe he'd judged his dad too harshly. He'd had hope for a split second that his dad was worth all the effort he'd put into winning his approval. "He cheated for years before they caught him." He waited for the question again, for her to ask again whether he'd cheated.

But she didn't. She was quiet, and his tension began to rise, wondering what she was thinking. He'd learned long ago not to be held back by what anyone thought of him, to tell people to fuck off if they judged him, but as he sat there with Noelle in his arms, he became increasingly tense, waiting for her response. He realized that he needed her to believe his innocence. No one except Bunny and Brody fully believed his innocence, and suddenly, he needed Noelle to. He didn't know why, but he did.

With every bit of his broken, trampled soul.

Chapter 9

F INALLY, SHE SPOKE. "Getting you kicked off the tour for cheating sounds like something that Octavia, or those other two cowboys would do. Why are you so sure it wasn't them?"

Her question shocked him, making him realize that she hadn't even bothered to wonder about his innocence. She'd accepted it automatically, and had already moved on to figuring out who might have done it. *She believed his innocence.* Sudden emotion rushed through him, a surging turmoil of feelings, and a tightness in his chest. "Because Jesse was convinced it was attempted murder. Murder is different than cheating. Octavia and the others want money, not blood on their hands. They wouldn't do it."

Noelle heard the conviction in his voice, and her heart ached for him. He wanted to believe in Octavia, in the men who were his peers. Despite all the betrayal, both by Octavia and the tour, Wyatt needed to prove to himself he hadn't been completely wrong in believing in them at one time.

She wanted him to be right, but at the same time, she'd written too many mysteries not to know that the most devastating betrayal possible was by those you loved, those you believed in the most. Yeah, in fiction that was the best kind of bad guy to write, but in real life, it happened as well, much too often.

"You believe me, don't you?" His question was quiet, almost a whisper, a question he didn't really want to ask, that he was half hoping she didn't hear.

She heard. Not only did she hear the question he posed, but she also heard the yearning in his soul, the one that needed someone to believe in him. So, she twisted around in the saddle and looked at him, at his icy blue eyes, at the shadows on his face. She saw the man who lived with honor, who had fought for everything against the shadows that weren't his. Her heart turned over, and she set her hands on either side of his face. "I have absolutely no doubt that you are a man of integrity and honor. I don't believe for even a second that you cheated. We'll figure out what happened, and we will clear your name. For good."

He searched her face. "It's impossible to clear my name for good," he said. "It's too tainted. But I'm not walking away. People think I shouldn't ride this weekend, that I shouldn't be back. Screw that. I'm back." But his voice was tense, too tense, and she knew what he was thinking.

"But you can't get your groove, right? Like I can't find my muse?"

He sighed. "Yeah. I need to win the next three events to have a shot at winning the title."

"Which will shut them all up, right?"

He laughed. "Yeah, well, something like that."

"You can't find your rhythm, and I can't find my muse, and we both desperately need to." She settled back against him, sounding thoughtful. "Maybe we were meant to find each other and help each other pull our talents out of the swamp they've sunk into."

Wyatt rested his chin on her shoulder, thinking about that as they neared the ranch. "So, solving my attempted murder might help us both. You can turn my life into a best-selling novel, and I can be freed from the burden and focus on riding, not the bullshit."

"Maybe." She ran her hands over his wrists, feeling lighter than she had in a long time. "I'm not going to lie. In a weird, kind of macabre sort of way, I think the idea of solving your almost murder sounds like fun. But I'm an author, so I'm totally weird and insane like that."

He laughed. "Yeah, well, I'm a bull rider, so I'm off the charts mentally anyway. You have to be to ride." He held out his hand to her. "Let's make a deal. Let's channel our insanity, find the scumbag who tried to get me killed, and then go kick some ass in our professional careers. Deal?"

She set her hand in his, feeling happier than she had in a long time. "I can't believe you aren't horrified by how much fun I think this sounds."

"I can't believe you aren't horrified by the fact you're riding a horse with a guy who has a murderer hunting him, who plans to go against all common sense and ride bulls for the next month just so he can get a shot at a title no one wants him to have."

She smiled as they touched hands. "I was kind of horrified that you were willing to risk death when I first met you–"

"You mean, about an hour ago?"

She laughed. "Yes, about then. I was kind of horrified because I spent three years watching my husband die a horrible death, but I see now that it's your fire and your willingness not to care about death that makes you live." She ran her hand over his wrist, noting how freaking strong it was. He was strong because he wasn't afraid to die, to fail, to crash and burn. "To really live, you have to let the fire inside you burn, don't you?"

She felt his nod against her shoulder, as he flipped her hand over and enfolded it in his. "Yeah, you do. If you kill the fire that makes you who you are, you're dead already. Even if the rest of the entire damn world thinks you should shut it down, you still gotta go forward."

Her heart tightened at his words, and she suddenly realized that that was exactly what she had done for so long. She'd been afraid to live, afraid to be happy, afraid to dance in her life, afraid that to do so would insult David, what he'd gone through, what he'd suffered. How could she be happy when he was gone? When he had suffered? When his brother was teetering on the edge?

God, she wanted to live with fierce passion. She wanted to not worry or obsess about how things might turn out. She wanted to unleash the fire that she'd killed off so long ago. She wanted to not be afraid to be who she was anymore. Ever.

"Barn's up ahead." He pointed past her, and she looked ahead to see two large barns in front of her. Both looked like they'd been well-used, with their faded wood and peeling paint, but they looked sturdy and solid. Functional, not flashy, and she liked them. It felt more her than spending her nights in a fancy restaurant, worrying about whether the linens had been properly pressed, or whether the food was plated with enough aplomb to make even the most discerning diner sigh with appreciation.

She didn't want fancy plates. She didn't care. She wanted fire and life and passion.

"The barn on the left, the big one, is for the bulls. Bunny has a small breeding operation, but she has two great bulls that are turning out some great stock. The barn on the right is for the horses. Can't have a ranch without horses, right?" As he spoke, he turned his head toward the destination in question. "See the house on the hill? That's Bunny's place. That's where you'll be."

Noelle looked up the hill at the white ranch house perched above the barns. It was also old and somewhat faded, but there were brightly colored flowers decorating it. It was a small ranch house, with a huge deck on the right side, looking over the property, including both barns and the two corrals up ahead. She imagined herself sitting out there with her computer, and something softened inside her. Something that felt good. Something that felt strong. Something that felt like *her.* "It's perfect," she whispered.

"Perfect?" Wyatt peered past her, frowning. He'd never considered the house as anything other than a functional building. He narrowed his eyes, trying to see what had put that reverence in Noelle's voice. "The flowers?"

"Everything." Her fingers tightened around his wrists. "I love it. I love this whole place. It's amazing."

Now, that, he understood. He looked across the property as he directed his horse to the barn. He'd spent many, many hours on that property, helping out Bunny, making sure things ran correctly. The place was a nugget, a sliver of gold that just needed the right hand to make it happen. For a split second, he thought of Brody's comment that he should take over when Bunny sold it, but he quickly dismissed it.

He was a bull rider, and he needed to be free to do what he did best, not bound to a ranch that would trap him. So, he simply shrugged. "Yeah, it's a good place."

"Good? It's great." Her voice faded as they neared the

barn. "Where do you stay?"

Wyatt nodded to the northwest. "Bunk house behind the bull barn."

She looked over at it, and he followed her glance to the small, two room building. It was small, simple, spartan. Took care of his needs just fine. But as he looked at it, he had a sudden vision of Noelle walking in there, of the way that she would light up that place, making the old building start to breathe in a way it hadn't breathed in a very long time.

Shit. He wanted her, didn't he? He didn't just want her. He needed her. He needed her light. Her energy. Her lack of judgment. He needed the way she made him feel, like he was the breath that made her heart beat.

Bunny would kick his ass if he messed with her guest. Swearing, he directed Lightning into the barn, tightening his arm around Noelle's waist as they rode straight in. He needed to get off that horse, get Noelle up to the house, and disentangle himself from the spell she was casting on him.

He reined his mount to a halt, then swung his leg back to dismount, wanting nothing more than to get away from the temptation that Noelle posed...because a deeper part of him didn't want to move away from her for even a second.

His boots thudded on the wood floor, and he instinctively reached up to help her down. He caught her around the waist as she slid off, steadying her as she lost her balance. Her hips were warm and curvy beneath his palms, and temptation coursed through him.

Swearing, he dropped his hands and stepped back just as she turned to face him. Her cheeks were glistening with rain, her hair plastered to her head, her face pale from the cold. But it was her eyes, always her eyes, that caught his attention. He swore, and moved a step toward her, just enough to trace his fingers along her jaw. "Your eyes are incredible. So much sadness, so much strength, so much courage. So much...realness."

She looked up at him, not moving away from him. "I've felt numb for so long," she whispered, "but in such a short time, you've made my heart start to beat again. I feel like I'm coming to life again, or maybe for the first time ever." She put her hand on his, holding his fingers to her face. "Thank you for that, Wyatt."

He laughed softly. "Sweetheart, you're restoring my faith in humanity. I'm the one who owes you." His smile faded as his gaze settled on her face. The air between them seemed to thicken, and suddenly he knew that despite his best intentions, he was going to kiss her.

Right then.

Right there.

Regardless of whether it was the proper thing to do.

He was going to kiss her, because he was pretty damn certain that if he didn't, his heart would never beat right again.

Chapter 10

W YATT WAS GOING to kiss her.

Noelle's heart started to hammer when she saw the expression on Wyatt's face, and her stomach trembled. She hadn't had a first kiss in years, and she hadn't wanted one.

Until now. Until Wyatt. Until he'd touched her cheek with his fingers, and made her feel alive again.

He waited, and she knew he was giving her a chance to stop him.

She didn't.

After a moment, understanding dawned in his eyes, a realization that she wasn't going to make him stop. A small smile of satisfaction curved the corners of his insanely sexy mouth, and his fingers tightened on her jaw. "My breath of sunshine," he whispered, as he bent his head and leaned toward her.

Noelle's heart leapt the moment she felt his lips touch hers. His kiss was a tender, sweet, decadent caress that flooded her with emotions. Need. Longing. Desire. And a sense of being treasured, as if she were the most precious soul he could ever hold in his arms. He was strong and rugged, a powerhouse that didn't need anything from her...and yet he still wanted her. His fingers stroked along her jaw as he kissed her, his lips evoking swirls of pleasure as she surrendered to him.

With a low groan, he slid his free arm around her waist, drawing her against him. Her belly pressed against his belt buckle, the heat from his body pouring into her. His hold on her was solid and strong, a wall of support that made her feel safe, not threatened, despite his strength.

He angled his head, deepening the kiss, asking for more. With a low sigh of pleasure, she couldn't contain, she kissed him back, allowing herself to melt into his embrace.

It felt so amazing to be kissed by him. To be kissing him back. To feel her body against his solid, muscular frame. To have the raw fire of his being igniting her through his kiss, his touch, and his body.

"God, you taste incredible," he whispered against her lips, just before taking her mouth again, in a kiss that was more about raw need than sweet tenderness.

Heat roared through her, and she slid her arms behind his neck, drawing him closer, needing more from him, from his kiss, from the unapologetic vitality coursing through him. His hands settled on her hips, and then slid down, over her butt. Need hummed through her, a need so strong that her entire body vibrated with it. She wanted him. Needed him. Not just a kiss. She needed everything.

"Noelle." The way he said her name was pure seduction, and, not breaking the kiss, he backed her up with his body, until her back hit the wall of the barn. He pressed his body against her, deepening the kiss until she couldn't think, until she was consumed by the essence of him. Were they going to make love in the barn? Right there? Still in muddy, wet clothes?

Her fingers went to his belt, and she knew the answer was yes. *Yes. YES.*

The lights suddenly went on, a blinding light that made her flinch. Wyatt swore, lifting his head to look behind him...and then he went rigid, his hands tightening on her hips. "Son of a bitch," he muttered.

He whipped around with lightning speed, shoving Noelle behind him, shielding her with his body.

Noelle froze, her heart hammering in sudden fear. Her hands clenched in his shirt, and she leaned to her right to peer around his shoulder.

Standing in the doorway to the barn, wearing jeans, a white cowboy hat, and a leather jacket, was a woman who had a body meant for sinning, and a wardrobe meant for luxury. She was looking right at Wyatt, and from the look of pure venom on her face, Noelle knew exactly who she was. She didn't need to hear Wyatt say it.

But he did anyway. One word that made chills shudder through her. "Octavia."

The moment Wyatt saw the expression on Octavia's face, he knew he'd made a major mistake. He'd underestimated her a thousand-fold. She was beyond pissed at him. Pissed enough to try to murder him? Shit. She looked like it...which scared the living hell out of him for one reason, and one reason only: the woman standing behind him.

His entire body went into high alert, and his left hand tightened on Noelle's hip, keeping her behind him. His right hand hung loosely beside his body, ready to fight, ready to defend, ready to protect her. Before this moment, before Noelle, he'd wanted to know one thing: who the hell had tripped his ride, and why. He would have grilled Octavia relentlessly until he had answers.

But with Noelle behind him, he could think of only one thing: defusing the situation and getting Octavia the hell away from Noelle. "What's up, Tav?" He kept his voice as neutral as possible, trying to keep the hostility out of his voice, wanting to give her nothing to play off of.

"You told Jesse Knight I tried to kill you?" Octavia's gaze kept flicking behind him, clearly trying to get a good look at Noelle. "You get me fired from my job, wreck my career, and now try to get a murder rap pinned on me?" Her voice was hard. Ice cold. Ruthless.

Wyatt swore under his breath. "Jesse asked me who hated me. I said you did. Was I wrong?" He couldn't believe he'd fallen for Tav. His entire body recoiled at the sight of her now. Even her body, which pretty much every male who'd ever met her coveted, made his gut turn over. Noelle was so much more beautiful, with her deeply emotional eyes, the beauty of her heart, the way her body filled out her jeans, and her complete honesty about who she was.

Noelle. She was the one he wanted. And she was in danger because of him.

Fuck.

Emotion flashed in Octavia's eyes. "No. You weren't wrong. I do hate you. I trusted you, and you turned me in."

He blinked. "*You* trusted *me?* You tried to get me to give up the championship so your boyfriend could win, and you could take home cash." Just saying the words made that same, deep sense of betrayal settle in his gut. It was more than that she'd been sleeping around on him. It was that he thought she believed he was a good guy, and in truth, she'd seen him as nothing more than the son of a famous cheater, just like every other bastard who'd refused to believe in him.

Noelle put her hand on his lower back, jerking his attention from the moment and back to her. Heat poured through him, a crazy, intense kind of warmth that enveloped him, somehow penetrating the icy coldness that gripped him so tightly. Suddenly, Tav's betrayal didn't hold so much strength, because he knew Noelle believed in him.

This woman he barely knew somehow was willing to see the truth in him that no one else could see. From one simple touch, Noelle had pulled him back from the edge, from the places he'd gone his whole life when someone had seen him as the cheater he'd never been, the cheater whose blood ran in his veins.

The tension inside him settled, and he looked at Octavia, suddenly feeling pity for her, instead of contempt and anger. "You chose your own path, Tav. I had nothing to do with it."

Anger flickered in her eyes. "You walked away from me, instead of helping. We could have been so much."

"No. There was nothing we could have been together." Wyatt didn't want to hear it. He didn't want to go there. Not anymore. "Walk away, Tav. Let it go."

"Let it go?" Anger flashed in her eyes. "You're the one who sent Jesse Knight to my office, asking questions that don't look so good to my bosses. They put me on leave, Wyatt. Suspended, pending investigation. For *murder*. What the hell? You really think I'm capable of murder?"

There was something in her voice, a desperation, a pain that broke through his walls. He suddenly saw the same shadows she lived under, being judged for who she was and what she had done. He knew in that second that she hadn't tried to kill him. "You didn't do it, did you?"

All the fury went out of her. "No," she whispered. "I didn't. I would never have tried to kill you, Wyatt, I swear."

He knew she was telling the truth, but there was something else in her eyes, something that made him tense. "Who did?"

Her gaze flicked away from him for a split second, but it was long enough to reveal the truth. He tensed again. "You know, don't you?" he pressed. "You know who did it?"

"I..." She glanced toward the door, and suddenly Wyatt knew they weren't alone. And from the look on Octavia's face, he knew that he was in trouble. Big trouble. Big *fucking* trouble.

But he wasn't prepared for who walked in.

Chapter 11

NOELLE FROZE WHEN she saw a man emerge from the shadows into the aisle of the barn. He was lean and wiry. A small man with glasses, and the kind of shifty eyes that made fear creep down her spine. There was no way he had the physique to ride a bull, but there was an ominous presence that clung to him, a raw, insidious power that hung over him like a poisoned aura. He nodded at Wyatt as he walked in. "Wyatt."

Wyatt tensed, his hand digging into Noelle's hip. "You?"

The man raised his brows. "Good evening, Wyatt."

"What the hell? You tried to murder me for this ranch? Is that what this is about?" Wyatt sounded incredulous, but from the hard expression on the man's face, Noelle had a feeling Wyatt was right that this was the one who had tried to kill him, but why? Who was this guy?

The man said nothing, and she felt Wyatt tense. He took a deep breath, and when he spoke, he sounded calm and steady, clearly trying to deescalate the situation. "I'm not planning on buying this ranch, Nathan." Wyatt's hand tightened on Noelle's hip. "You can have it."

"It doesn't matter. Bunny won't sell it to me. My own aunt won't sell me the land that should be mine by inheritance."

Awareness dawned on Noelle. This was Bunny's nephew, and he wanted the ranch. Why on earth would anyone want a ranch so much that they would murder for it? That made no sense.

Nathan's face was dark, almost twisted with hate as he glared at Wyatt. "I spent twenty years being nice to the old bat so that I'd get what I was owed, but she won't sell it to me. She doesn't want a resort property, even though it would make us all rich. She wants to remain true to the spirit of the place. Horses. A ranch. All that bullshit."

"I am not planning on buying the ranch," Wyatt said again, his voice calm and steady. Only the tightness of his grip on Noelle's hip indicated how tense he was.

Nathan circled closer, like a predator stalking his prey, which she found so creepy that she would definitely put it in her next book, assuming she didn't die. Oh, God. Was she going to die? Who would kill over a ranch? That was absurd, right?

Nathan sneered at Wyatt. "I saw Bunny's will two months ago. If she dies, you get it. You get the whole damn place. So, I can't kill her as long as you're around."

The casual way he referenced killing his aunt made fear congeal in Noelle's stomach. Oh, God. Seriously? With all the psychos she'd written about, she had truly failed to do justice to how damn scary it was to be trapped by one.

"She never believed all the rumors about you being a cheat," Nathan continued. "I worked hard as hell, and so did Octavia, to spread those rumors. I got the whole tour labeling you as a cheat, and Bunny still worships you." Bitterness raked across his face. "You're a damned cheat, and you still get the ranch." Then, he reached behind him, grabbed something from his waistband, and raised a gun. "Unless you die before she does. Then I'm all the family she has left, and it's mine."

Wyatt went utterly still, and Noelle froze. She couldn't breathe. Her breath seemed to freeze in her lungs. There was an actual *gun* pointed at them. A *gun.* Dear God. How was this possible?

She'd spent three years with David, trying to help him deal with the fact he was dying. She'd been so certain she understood what it was like to face death, to know what it was like to understand one's mortality, but nothing in her life, or her experience with David, had prepared her for the shock to her body as she stared at that gun.

A thousand thoughts and memories flooded her...and every one was about the life she'd let slip away. About giving up on living, on loving, both herself and others, because she'd been so caught up in duty, or obligation, or all of the noise that life had hammered her with for so long.

Dear God. She was going to die, just like David. Except David had lived fully while he'd been alive. He'd opened his restaurant. He'd saved his brother. He'd married the woman he loved. What had she done? Rotted away for the last year under the weight of guilt and obligation, trying to live David's life for him...not her life. His. Which he had already done, to the best of his ability.

And now...there was a man pointing a gun at her. A man who had done his best to sabotage Wyatt's career, and tried to kill him a few months ago, and now... God, now he looked like he was ready to finish it.

Nathan wasn't bluffing. She could see the fury, the ice-cold anger in his eyes, the absolute sense of entitlement. The ranch belonged to him, and Wyatt was the one standing in his way.

Wyatt.

Suddenly, she forgot about herself. She forgot about her own mortality. Everything was obliterated by the thought of the man still shielding her with his body, the one who had just found out that the rumors that had robbed him of a career he was due had been carefully orchestrated to ruin him.

Wyatt still hadn't moved, but his fingers were digging into her hip almost painfully, the only indication that he'd heard anything Nathan had said. "Noelle," he said softly. "I think you should leave. Nathan and I have some things to talk about."

Her heart tightened. He was trying to get her to safety. He wasn't reacting to anything Nathan had said. He'd somehow managed to stay completely calm, and she knew it was for her sake. How sweet was that? He was every bit as heroic as she'd thought he was.

Nathan didn't lower the gun, but his gaze flicked to Noelle. "Who are you?"

"She's a guest at the ranch," Wyatt answered. "Bunny did a house swap with her, and she just arrived today. She has nothing to do with it. Let her walk away."

Nathan's gaze flicked to her, and she saw the hesitation in his eyes. He didn't want to kill her, a random stranger. Thank God. A murderer with morals, a line he wouldn't cross. Yay for her, right? "Is that true?" he asked her.

Before Noelle could emphatically confirm that yes, indeed, she didn't need to be killed today, Octavia interrupted. "Wyatt was kissing her. I saw them. He had her pinned against the wall and they were getting it on."

Noelle felt the blood drain from her face as Nathan's face darkened. "You fucking liar, Wyatt. Anyone who matters to you becomes fair game." He aimed the gun at Noelle. "You shacked up with the wrong guy, sweetheart. Too bad for you."

Noelle's throat suddenly felt so dry she couldn't talk. "Please let me go. Wyatt's telling the truth. I mean, yeah, he kissed me, but I don't know him." If she could just get out of there, she could call 9-1-1, and–

Wyatt's fingers tightened on her hip. "Nathan, don't make it worse for yourself. Let her go."

"No." Nathan's face darkened. "Fuck you, Wyatt. Just fuck you." He nodded at Octavia. "Get the rope from the tack room." He pointed the gun at Wyatt. "You two, into that stall. Now."

Noelle's heart pounded. Rope? Stall? Wyatt took her elbow and began to move her toward the stall. He was moving slowly, and his body was tense. She knew he was looking for an opening, but there wasn't one, not yet. The guy had a freaking gun. What kind of opening could they get against a *gun?*

As they moved across the aisle toward the stall, she saw a stack of metal cans outside the main door. Gasoline? Dear God, he was going to burn down the barn with them in it. Destroy the ranch and kill the heir at the same time. Why did murder seem so much more fun when she was writing about it in her cute, little condo, than it did when she was faced with it in real life? Honestly. This was not at all the same thing! "Wyatt–"

"I see the gasoline," he whispered.

Noelle felt like she was going to throw up as they moved toward the stall. Behind Nathan, Wyatt's horse had wandered off, nosing through the hay bales at the far end of the aisle in search of a snack. He was near the door, close enough to get out if the barn started burning. Would he leave, or would they all go down? Because it was bad enough for Wyatt and her to die, but a horse, too? That was just wrong on a whole other level.

Anger on behalf of Lightning pulsed through her, chasing away the fear. Burning to death? Really? What kind of asinine plot was that? It was melodramatic, and, quite frankly, much too brutal for her cozy mysteries, which meant it was much too brutal for *real life*. For God's sake, this needed to end now. "Nathan," she said, impressed with how she managed to keep her voice from trembling. "You haven't done anything bad yet. If you walk away, you're still free. It's not worth it over a ranch, and you'll get caught. They always do." Well, not always, but he would be a pretty obvious suspect once the fire marshal figured out it was arson.

Nathan's face was impassive as he watched them. "Shut up, bitch. I don't give a shit what you have to say. You lost the right to have me care when you kissed this cheat."

Okay, that was *it*. She was officially pissed now. "He's not a cheat!" She snapped the words before she could stop herself. "You can spread all the rumors you want, but the reason your aunt believes in Wyatt is because she can see the truth. He's a good man, and killing him will never change that!"

Wyatt swore under his breath when he heard Noelle defend him. Fear ripped through him, a raw terror for her safety. He caught her arm and pulled her behind him. "Don't defend me," he muttered under his breath. "I don't need it."

She glared at him. "Yes, you do. You haven't defended yourself your whole life, have you? You just ride silently, hoping that if you win, people will forget about the rumors. Why don't you just tell them?"

"Because they won't believe me, and I'm not wasting my breath." They were near the doorway to the stall now, and Wyatt could see Octavia coming back down the aisle toward them, several ropes in her hand. Hell. If Nathan got them in the stall, there would be no way out.

He had no doubt that Nathan meant to kill them both. Wyatt had an idea, a sliver of an opportunity that might give Noelle time to get away. He knew it wouldn't be enough to save them both, but it would get Noelle out of there.

Noelle. His gut tightened. She'd mouthed off to a psychopath with a gun to defend him. What was she thinking? She shouldn't have done it, but at the same time, it felt so damn good, good in a way he could barely register, to have her defending him openly, and without fear of reprisal. Just because she believed in him and wouldn't sit back silently when she could right a wrong.

What the hell? He didn't even understand that. There was a gun pointing at her and a problem that wasn't hers, yet she'd made it hers by standing up for him.

And for that, he would do whatever it took to make her safe.

He caught her arms. "Resist me," he whispered under his breath. "Resist going in the stall."

She looked at him sharply, then stopped in place. "I'm not going in there," she announced. "There's no way that I'm going to roll over so that some jerk can kill me easily."

He almost chuckled at the stubbornness on her face. He could feel her trembling, but no one would guess it from looking at her. "Don't make it difficult," he said, loud enough for Nathan to hear. "We can still talk him out of it." He wrapped his arm around her waist, as if he were trying to force her into the stall. The action brought her up against him, close enough for him to whisper under his breath into her ear. "When I say go, run for the doors and don't look back," he muttered, as he continued to make a show of trying to push her into the stall. With her resisting back, it wasn't hard to make a scene.

Her body was warm and soft against his, vulnerable and real, making fear congeal in his gut. He'd never been scared of death in his life, but he was absolutely scared shitless right now at the thought she could get hurt. "My truck is parked in back," he said softly, "and the keys are in the ignition. Drive like hell south and you'll reach a general store. Call the cops from there, and don't come back. Got it?"

"Let me go," she snapped, pushing at him. He wasn't sure if the resistance was for Nathan's benefit, or if she didn't like his plan.

Too bad if she didn't like it. He was getting her the hell out of there. "Got it?" he asked quietly, locking his arms around her waist, a move that brought her tightly against him.

She looked at him. "You come with me," she whispered.

"Won't work that way," he said. "Got it?"

She searched his face.

"We will both die," he snapped, barely able to keep his voice quiet, the fear for her safety was so great. He knew Nathan would believe the false struggle for only so long. "Get the hell out. Got it?"

She looked at him for a long moment, and finally nodded. Relief rushed through him, and for a moment, he paused, sliding his fingers along her jaw. Her skin was so soft, so beautiful, so flawless. "You're the sunshine that I've never seen in my life, until now," he whispered. "Never stop pouring your light into the world. Promise?"

Tears filled her eyes, but she nodded. "Don't die," she whispered. "He doesn't deserve it."

"I know, babe. I know. But sometimes that's the way life is." Unable to stop himself, he bent his head and kissed her. A slow, short kiss that said all the words he didn't know how to say. A thank you for showing him the things he'd never been able to see before this moment. He pulled back, searching her face. He saw confusion and warmth, a kindness that made his heart turn over. He was vaguely aware of Octavia's snort of disgust, and Nathan's command to hurry up, but he didn't care.

All that mattered was Noelle.

He pulled back, and for one endless, agonizingly short moment, he simply stared at her. He saw in her eyes the future that he'd never hoped for, the hope he'd never dared have. On her face, he saw something similar, a warmth directed right at him that seemed to sink deep into his heart...and suddenly, he didn't want to die either.

He wanted a chance with this woman. A chance to see what could happen.

But it wasn't a risk he would take if it meant endangering her.

There would be time only to save her. Not both of them. He had to make the choice. "I wish I had more time with you," he said softly.

Tears filled her eyes. "Not again," she whispered. "God, not again."

He knew she was referring to the man she'd loved and lost, and his heart turned over. Somehow, in the short time they'd been together, she'd put Wyatt in the same place in her heart. Son of a bitch. If he died, it would hurt her.

Screw that.

She didn't get hurt twice.

For her sake, he'd have to live. Resolution flooded him, and he turned toward Nathan and Octavia, his mind rapidly assessing his options. Octavia was furious, but his gut told him she wouldn't kill him. He had to bank on that. Was it worth the risk of being wrong, if it gave him a chance to save his own life?

He felt the way Noelle's fingers were digging into his back, and he knew the answer was yes. For Noelle, he'd do whatever it took to try to stay alive.

Chapter 12

I F WYATT WAS going to stay alive, he was going to have to come up with another plan. Swearing, he looked past Nathan and Octavia to his horse, who was munching on the hay by the door.

"A few more feet," he said to Noelle, moving her further toward the stall door, changing the angle slightly. Could he really pull off saving both of them? He wasn't sure, but he had to try.

She let him move her, and he whistled softly under his breath. Lightning's head snapped up and he turned to look at Wyatt, his ears perked. His tail stopped swishing, and his attention focused fully on Wyatt, waiting for the next command.

One chance. They would have one chance. Wyatt moved a few more inches to the left, trying to get in the best spot. Octavia's eyes narrowed, and she looked over her shoulder. He swore, aware that Octavia knew how he trained his horses.

It was now...or never. He whistled sharply, two quick blasts, and Lightning exploded into motion, launching into a full gallop, straight at Wyatt. Nathan whirled around, and Wyatt shoved Noelle toward the door. "Go!"

She took off in a sprint, and Wyatt launched himself at Nathan. Lightning plowed into Nathan, knocking him off balance just as Wyatt reached him. Wyatt tackled the other man, reaching for his gun as Lightning thundered past.

There was a deafening blast, and Wyatt gasped as pain shot through his hip. Jesus. He'd been shot?

"Wyatt?" Noelle's horrified gasp ripped through him.

She was still there. Shit. He had to give her time to get away.

Adrenaline rushed through his body, and Wyatt rolled to his side as Nathan started to scramble to his feet. Wyatt tackled him and shoved him to the side, slamming him into the side of the stall. Nathan's head hit first, and he went limp, collapsing on the ground. Wyatt sank beside him, his hand on his hip, gasping for breath.

"Get off him."

He turned his head and saw Octavia pointing the gun at him. Her hands were shaking, and her face was ashen. *Hell.* "Put the gun down, Tav," Wyatt said, keeping his voice steady. "You haven't done anything yet. Let him take the heat."

She shook her head. "Get in the stall, Wyatt."

Wyatt felt Nathan move slightly, and realized the other man was starting to regain consciousness. Swearing, he grabbed Nathan under the arms and staggered to his feet. "I'm putting him in the stall, Tav. You'll have to shoot me to stop me." He intentionally used her nickname, trying to create a bond.

She raised the gun, aiming it at his chest. "I won't let the man I love go to prison. Put him down, Wyatt. Put him down."

Nathan groaned, and Wyatt knew they were almost out of time. Shit–

Movement behind Octavia suddenly caught his eye. He had a split second to see Noelle reach for a small fire extinguisher hanging by the door, before he jerked his gaze off her. Shit. What was she doing?

He couldn't let Octavia turn around and see Noelle. Swearing under his breath, he began dragging Nathan toward the stall again. "You're better than this, Tav. You're brilliantly talented at journalism, and you don't need to be stuck in this life, trying to steal to get money. You can do more. Don't let him drag you down."

"I mean it, Wyatt! Put him down!" She pulled the trigger, and Wyatt jumped as the wood behind his left shoulder splintered.

Hell. She *was* willing to shoot him. Clearly, he wasn't as charming as he'd thought he was. He was going to have to work on that next time he was at the wrong end of a gun.

He saw movement behind her, but he didn't dare draw her attention to Noelle, so he kept his gaze on Octavia. Why the hell wasn't Noelle leaving?

Nathan twisted out of his grip suddenly, and Wyatt swore, knowing that it was over–

Fire extinguisher foam suddenly blasted Octavia in the back. She shrieked and turned around, and got it full in the face. Wyatt slammed his fist into Nathan's face, and hurled him into the stall. He slammed the latch shut, then leapt at Octavia as she stumbled, covering her face with her hands.

He snatched the gun from her hand and turned it on her. "Get down, Octavia."

She immediately dropped to her knees, coughing and gagging. Noelle was behind her in a split second, binding her wrists with the same rope that Octavia had been planning to use on them. Noelle grinned up at him, then looked behind him. Her face went stark in warning. "Nathan's coming–"

Wyatt grabbed the abandoned fire extinguisher and spun around just as Nathan opened the stall door. He hurled the extinguisher at him, catching him square in the chest, knocking him down. This time, Wyatt didn't give him a second chance to get up. He sprinted over with the rest of the rope, and tied him down.

It took only seconds to immobilize him, then Wyatt stepped back, leaving him trussed up like a calf in a roping event. He looked over at Noelle, and then grinned when he saw her standing over Octavia, looking incredibly pleased with herself. "You did great, Noelle."

She beamed at him. "Thanks. I really couldn't bring myself to brain her with the fire extinguisher, but my last book had a particularly soft-hearted villain, so I just did what she did and sprayed instead. It worked just like my research said it would. It was fun." Her smile faded as her gaze settled on his hip. "You're shot?"

The moment she said it, the pain came rushing back. Dizziness slammed into him, and Wyatt sank to his knees, pressing his hand to his hip. Noelle gasped and ran over, catching him as he started to slide to the ground. "I don't have cell service. Where's a phone?"

He bent over, bracing his hands on the floor as he fought for breath. His hip felt warm, and he could feel the blood seeping over his jeans. He'd had many significant injuries over the years, but never had he experienced anything like this. He gritted his jaw, fighting to shut off the pain. Son of a bitch. He'd ignored pain before, but he couldn't believe he'd been able to ignore the gunshot for so long.

Except he could believe it. Noelle's life had depended

on him, and a lifetime of ignoring pain had enabled him to save her, to save them. But now that the danger was over...*shit.*

"Wyatt! Where's the phone?"

He gritted his teeth, pressing his hand to the wound. "By the barn doors. I didn't bring mine. Too wet outside." He bowed his head, sinking to the floor as he heard Noelle talking to the operator. His vision began to blur and he swore. Too much blood loss. He had to stop it. Had to find a way. He tried to crawl over to the tack box by the stall, but his legs weren't working–

Noelle was suddenly by his side again, her hands on his shoulders. "Wyatt–"

"Get wraps from the tack box." He gave up trying to crawl and went down on his side. "White cotton. Need to stop the bleeding."

Noelle felt like her heart was going to stop when Wyatt collapsed on the ground. The blood stain was spreading across his stomach with a speed that was terrifying. How had he kept going when he was shot? The strength of his will was astonishing. Incredible. And not surprising.

She'd known he was strong from the moment she'd met him, but now she knew how strong he truly was, both physically and emotionally. He was the rock her soul had been searching for...and now she might lose him.

Fighting off tears, she raced over to a nearby trunk and opened it. Inside were an assortment of what looked like cloth diapers, which she knew were wraps for the horse's legs. She grabbed several and ran back to Wyatt, going down on her knees beside him.

Grimacing, she pressed one of the wraps against his hip, flinching when he let loose a string of profanities. "I thought cowboys were tough," she managed, her hands shaking violently. "And thoughtful. I mean, I just got through almost being murdered, and I need to collapse in emotional anguish now that it's over, and you're not giving me a chance to do that."

He closed his eyes, his face ashen. "I'm a cheating ass," he muttered. "Never said I was a good guy."

His words made her heart ache. "You're not a cheater," she whispered. "Stop labeling yourself. It's over, Wyatt. Don't you realize it's over?"

His eyes flickered open, and she saw that his ice blue eyes were darker now, richer, more complex. "It's not over, babe. It'll never be over."

Her heart sank, and she bent over him, bringing her face close to his. "It's over only if you let it be over. You have to let the past go." As she said it, she thought of David, of Joel, of the restaurant, and she knew she was speaking the truth. Just as Wyatt had to let go of the legacy his father had left him, so did she need to let go of the burden she'd taken on after David's death. "I want to live, Wyatt. I want to truly live. Don't you? Not be trapped by a past full of shadows."

Wyatt searched her face, her beautiful face full of pain and loss and courage...and hope. He saw hope in her eyes, a flash of light that made his own heart start to beat again, a heart that had stopped beating so long ago, long before he'd been shot. He reached up, brushing his finger over her cheeks. "All this time, I thought that winning the championship would make me able to breathe again. I was wrong. It was you."

She smiled. "And a gunshot wound."

He shook his head. "No, it was worrying that you were going to get hurt. It was seeing you defend me against Nathan, despite the gun. You're brave, you don't give a shit what people think, and you made me care if I lived for the first time in my life, because I wanted to stay alive for you." Shit. He couldn't believe he'd just said that aloud.

But when her face softened, he was glad he had. "I'm so glad you did, Wyatt."

His eyelids started to feel too heavy to stay open, and his head fell back on the hard floor. "Noelle?"

"Stay with me, Wyatt. The medics will be here soon."

He knew he was going to lose consciousness any second. He didn't know if he was going to come back. He knew he hadn't known her long enough to feel what he was feeling, to say what he wanted to say, but he was going to say it anyway, because he knew in his gut he was right. He'd lived long enough to see truth when he saw it, and he wasn't going to hide from it. "You saved me, Noelle. Not just my life, but my heart. For that, I will always love you." The words felt right as he said them. She'd broken through the walls in his heart the moment he'd seen her trying to claw her way up that muddy embankment, laughing in amusement. When she'd believed in him when no one else had, she'd won his loyalty forever. And when she'd let him see the real her, her tears, her courage, and her grief, he'd fallen in love with her, completely and irrevocably.

He felt the touch of her lips against his, a featherlight sensuality that went straight into his heart. "You saved me right back, Wyatt, and for that, I will always love you."

He smiled, her words wrapping around his heart. "Just so you know," he muttered, fighting against the lethargy trying to take him, "I'm going to pursue you like a coyote after a rabbit as soon as I can stand up again, so if that doesn't sound good to you, then you better hightail it back east before I get out of the hospital."

He'd give her one last chance, one last opportunity to claim a life without him. One last chance to walk away from the man everyone else thought was a cheater.

But she laughed softly and pressed a kiss to his cheek. "I bet you'd look good running across the Oregon plains in hot pursuit. I think I'll stay around and see if I'm right."

He smiled, his body relaxing at her words. She'd be there when he woke up, and then...yeah...then it was going to get good.

Chapter 13

N UMBER ONE.
Number one.
Noelle hung up the phone, unable to stop the tears from streaming down her face. *Number one.* God, how her life had changed–

Footsteps sounded on the front porch, but before she could wipe away the tears, the front door opened. In walked Wyatt, with a new saddle slung over his shoulder. His limp from being shot fourteen months ago was finally gone, and he was as lean and fit as he'd ever been. Behind him was Brody Hart, who was carrying what looked like a large, white cake box.

The minute Wyatt saw her face, he dropped the saddle and strode right over to her. "What's wrong, sweetheart? What happened?" His voice was so tender, so sweet, so concerned that she wanted to cry even harder.

She put her hands on his cheeks, his whiskers prickling her fingers. "How is it that I got so lucky to have you?"

He grinned. "It's a team win, babe." Then he wiped his thumb across her cheeks. "What's wrong? Why isn't my bride smiling the day before her wedding?"

Brody cleared his throat. "I'll just take the cake into the kitchen then, and you can check it out when you're ready." He ducked past them, giving them privacy.

Wyatt didn't even spare his best friend a glance. His entire being was focused on Noelle, making her feel as treasured as he had every day for the last fourteen months. She smiled through her tears. "My agent just called. My new mystery...it hit the New York Times list at number one." *Number one.*

His face lit up, and he let out a loud whoop. "Hot damn, girl! I knew you could do it." He grabbed her around the waist and swung her in a circle, making her burst into laughter as she hung on to keep from flying across the room.

Noelle locked her arms around his neck, beaming up at him. His face was happy and light, a perfect reflection of the joy dancing in her own heart. She loved this man so much, and he poured his love into every moment of life.

Wyatt angled his hat back, then bent his head and kissed her, a beautiful, amazing kiss that made her heart melt every bit as much as it had the very first time he'd kissed her in the barn on that rainy night so long ago.

Noelle clung to him, pouring her love into the kiss, needing to connect with him, to open her heart to this wonderful man who had changed her life. Wyatt's arms locked around her waist, and she melted into his strong body, loving the feel of his muscled strength encasing her in a shield of his love and protectiveness.

After a long moment, and a kiss that consumed her entire being, he pulled back a tiny bit, just enough for her to see his face. "I'm so proud of you, Noelle," he said. "I knew that book was genius when I read it, and I knew the world would see its brilliance."

She sighed and rested her wrists on his shoulders, her hands still clasped behind his neck. "And I knew that you would win that championship. It was so amazing to see you win after all you'd been through."

It had been a difficult off-season, with his recovery from being shot, but Noelle had used that time to make sure the entire bull riding tour understood what Nathan had done to his reputation. By the time Wyatt stepped back into the chute on the first competition of the season, he'd had fans screaming his name, and cowboys vying for a chance to have his back.

And now, he held the title he had coveted for so long, despite all that had happened.

He grinned, a shit-eating grin that never seemed to leave his face. She knew that her cowboy would always have a little bit of rebel in him, a little bit of needing to bask in his awesomeness, and she was just fine with that. A tender-hearted cowboy with a heart of gold and just enough arrogance to accomplish anything he wanted sounded perfect for her.

"Yeah, I got my win," he agreed, "but now it's time to turn this ranch into the brilliant operation that Bunny never had time to turn it into. Speaking of Bunny, has she arrived yet? I know she's dying to meet the woman who finally tamed me."

"Tamed you?" Noelle grinned. "You will never be tamed, Wyatt, and I'd never change that. I love the rebel in you, and the rancher, and the lover, and the man who makes me feel like the most treasured woman in the entire world."

His smile faded and he slid his hand through her hair. "You are, you know. I would trade my life for yours any second of any day."

"I know." She wrinkled her nose. "You almost did once. Let's not do it again, okay?"

His face softened with love. "Deal." He pulled her against him and kissed her again, this time a decadent, sensual kiss that made her think of tousled sheets, moonlight, and secrets shared between lovers. Kate would be arriving in a couple hours with Joel, who had turned the restaurant into a five-star destination in Boston. Bunny would be there momentarily. Brody was waiting in the kitchen, and his entire family was going to be attending as well.

She'd found her home, her man, and her heart...and he had done the same. She smiled up at him. "I love you, Wyatt Parker, and I will love you forever."

He smiled back at her, brushing a lock of hair off her face. "And I love you right back, sweetheart, and I am counting the seconds until you become my wife." He lifted her hand and pressed a kiss to each knuckle. "Forever and always, my love. Forever and always."

About The Author

Hailed by J.R. Ward as a "paranormal star, "*New York Times* and *USA Today* bestselling author Stephanie Rowe is the author of more than forty-five novels, and she's a four-time nominee for the RITA® award, the highest award in romance fiction.

For a complete booklist, visit:
www.stephanierowe.com

Keep up with the latest Stephanie Rowe news on Facebook at
www.facebook.com/StephanieRoweBooks

On Twitter at StephanieRowe2

Or by signing up for her private newsletter at:
http://stephanierowe.com/connect.php

Also by Stephanie Rowe

PARANORMAL ROMANCE

HEART OF THE SHIFTER SERIES
Dark Wolf Rising
Dark Wolf Unbound
Dark Wolf Untamed (coming soon!)

SHADOW GUARDIAN SERIES
Leopard's Kiss

ORDER OF THE BLADE SERIES
Darkness Awakened
Darkness Seduced
Darkness Surrendered
Forever in Darkness
Darkness Reborn
Darkness Arisen
Darkness Unleashed
Inferno of Darkness
Darkness Possessed
Shadows of Darkness
Hunt the Darkness (2016)

NIGHTHUNTER SERIES
Not Quite Dead

ROMANTIC SUSPENSE

ALASKA HEAT SERIES
Ice
Chill
Ghost

YOUNG ADULT

ONCE UPON AN ENDING SERIES
The Fake Boyfriend Experiment
Ice Cream, Jealousy, and Other Dating Tips
The Truth About Thongs)
How to Date a Bad Boy
Pedicures Don't Like Dirt (Coming Soon!)
Geeks Can Be Hot (Coming Soon!)